MANHATTAN MOURNING

SEAN MATHIAS

MANHATTAN MOURNING

Brilliance Books

This first edition published by
Brilliance Books/Plain Edition 1988
Copyright 1988 © Sean Mathias

Editor: T. K. Light

ISBN 0946189 37 4

Cover illustration: Roy Trevelion

Typeset by A.K.M. Associates (U.K.) Ltd.,
Southall, Greater London.

Printed and bound by Woolnough Bookbinding,
Wellingborough, Northants.

Brilliance Books 14 Clerkenwell Green,
London EC1R 0DP

For Dana Sagalyn

MANHATTAN MOURNING

PART ONE

She stood waiting. Unsure. Opposite was the little square with its fountain, overlooked by the Plaza. She had been there. She had known the great comforts the hotel had to offer. She had been there often. She had used the comforts, the services. Accepted its luxury.

Now she stood looking up at the hotel, reminiscing, though untouched. It was not that she craved a suite at the Plaza. She knew the inside of many limousines. All the same. All suites. All interiors. Differing only in their shades of grey, navy and royal.

She had no yearning, simply recognition. Feeling familiar from afar. That was how she felt. She was reasonable. A woman who could use her reason.

"Rosemary," she started to think somewhere in her grey interior, but before the thought could form itself, before she could acknowledge any of the jumbled jungle of useless thoughts and thinkings that swim through every second of each endless waking sleeping day, she was driven towards the nearest bench.

She might have remained on that previous spot forever. How unreasonable that would have been. To have stood there, always waiting for nothing. In the moment before she had moved there had seemed little alternative. How unreasonable. Rosemary was a reasonable woman. A realistic woman.

She wondered why she suddenly felt the whole world was watching her. Everyone on Central Park staring, the whole of Fifth Avenue walking away from her with their heads turned towards her, every window in every block, every window in the Plaza Hotel, a concealed face lay in wait, hoping for that very second when she would shift her feet and move to another position. Then they would point and snigger, laugh behind their hands, seem shocked, appalled, anything, but everyone would notice.

If she dared to throw coins into the bare violin case of the really very good player the world would notice that too; they would comment. It all rang true but lacked reason. Rosemary was a confident, beautiful woman.

She had lived more fully in the past but she was in no state of dilapidation. Not falling apart at the seams. Not Rosemary, no. She had moved, and no-one had noticed. How stupid to have become this self-conscious. It happened, to the most confident. It had a way of happening. A rush of self-consciousness as one climbed, a new passenger, onto the already travelling bus. People would look and notice, yet no-one *really* noticed. Hardly anyone. An occasional person. It was for this reason she had moved.

A man had walked towards her, right up to her. He had even spoken, quite unevenly. It had broken her trance. He had meant no harm, he was unimportant, he might play no part in her future life. Still at that moment he existed, had stepped towards her. His black wig was comic, falling carelessly from his crown, concealing his shallow forehead, revealing tufts at the back of his neck. It was the blackest wig she'd ever seen. The blackest wig the world would ever know. His ploughed face lacked danger; he was forthright; wanting to thrust himself. It was harmless.

He wheeled a trolley of shopping bags, containing a large doll sitting on top of two model aeroplanes. His shirt and trousers were loud; burlesque. A sense of vulgarity. His mac was dirty, a greying impermeability. When he spoke he was garbled, unconvincing, silly. It diffused the initial threat. It was all quite harmless. Rosemary's three paces sent piercing signals and he did not pursue.

He set down his trolley and started addressing the unattentive square around her.

The man was easily diverted from his inarticulate spasms by a passing girl. Any girl would do. He pursued temporarily. Rosemary would allow herself to be amused by this for a time. That was reasonable enough. Besides, she was able to listen to the violinist. He was good. He was also young and handsome in an unfocussed way. Poetic.

There was another man, staring at her. He was tall, and seemed to stand with his crotch directed towards her. He too was handsome. European, Dutch, maybe Flemish. He didn't have the definite look of a Frenchman or an Italian. Short hair and strong eyes. She could only pretend not to notice. It was not alarming, not dangerous. His crotch was a possible excitement. There were interesting lines in his jeans. He was well arranged. Well endowed. She felt her lower lip drop slowly downward and she turned away feeling slightly filthy. It was the European who was filthy. Standing there with his legs straddled.

He actually carried a clutch-bag! It was tucked under the pit of his arm. The leather snuggling against his jerkin, pushing the hair of his armpit into his flesh, sweating, trapped sweat trickling onto his chest, his male breast. Rosemary, with good reason, hated mens' clutch-bags. They were not attractive. The line below his waist disappeared in her mind's eye. Lost forever. Everything about him was contained in that purse. His virility, body hair, bulges were all inside his handbag. He appeared more comic than the man with the doll. The poor old Wigman, on reflection, was more attractive, a more sympathetic person.

There were others. Some had settled. One man paid great attention to the violinist. Girls passed by. The Wigman pursued momentarily, then forgot. Couples held hands, exchanged words. None of them touched Rosemary. No-one else would notice her. She would sit for a while. She would stay. Maybe all day. Possibly all afternoon. It was early afternoon. The rest of the day belonged to anyone. Time was on Rosemary's side. She had no need to rush. No reason to panic. It wasn't frightening to have time. She was young, and beautiful. She had a great deal of time. She was not in trouble.

Without notice, as suddenly as she had arrived at that bench she was up. Up and off. Past the violinist. She gave him a dollar. An entire dollar bill. Let the world see that. Her concern was that it shouldn't blow away. That would be a pity. An unnecessary loss. A waste. It was unlikely to blow away. He would stop playing. He would start running. He would chase his rent.

Turning sharply, confidently into Fifth Avenue, she walked north. Past the bus stop where a short line waited. She would not wait. She never waited at bus stops. How strange to stand around. How empty. She got on buses when they happened to arrive.

At the bus stop was one particular creature. Alarming in appearance. Hair piled high, so high and perched above it, a gaudy canvas hat. A gardening hat. The make-up intense. Flared trousers. Lime green jacket. Gloves. And, clutching in one hand, a kit bag with the word KARATE printed boldly across it. Over the shoulder a handbag attached to a thick metal chain. Large links, wrapped tightly around knuckles.

Rosemary was forced to stop. Man, woman, almost monster. Rosemary pretended to wait for the bus. She stole sidelong glances at the aggressor. The person was frightening, frightened and frightful. Rosemary's stare could neither fool nor escape the creature who darted a fierce look; a look to scare Rosemary. Happily the bus arrived.

As the creature got on Rosemary watched; watched the bus sail away, down Fifth Avenue. It was best to forget this person. To forget the entire incident. She did. She was reasonable. The other person had been unreasonable.

Rosemary carried on walking. After all, she had made a bold decision to get up from the bench. Not to dwindle in the square. No approaching person had forced that. She had wanted to walk. The man with his testicles in a handbag had tired of her. Her lack of response. The Wigman was still there. He might stay there forever; if not he would often go there. He would always be somewhere.

Somewhere on Manhattan. Wig and all. The violinist she had paid. Paid for her entertainment. She owed him nothing. None of them anything. That was best. That way she was free to carry on with the afternoon.

She walked up Fifth Avenue. Not hurrying. There was nothing to hurry for. No pressures. She had time, and no need to work. Enough money to live. Just. The rent was paid, there was money for food and the cinema. She had two strong legs. They were long and beautiful. Not suntanned. The sun was unimportant. She liked it to shine but she did not need to sunbathe.

She was determined to dawdle. That, after all, was quite a different matter from dwindling on a park bench. That had become a waste of time. Dawdling up Fifth Avenue was using time to suit oneself.

It was May, it was warm, it was perfect. No clouds. A good day in early summer in New York City. Rosemary liked the city this way. It was comfortable, enjoyable. Strolling up Fifth Avenue she could dawdle over her life. Gently gather her thoughts. That was something she enjoyed doing. She was almost thirty. Not so very frightening. It made her feel quite happy. Being almost twenty had too many problems. Life was complicated then. Now one had more control. Life, somehow, was easier.

She had first come to New York City when she was twenty-two. Within three months she was the mistress of a fabulously rich and handsome industrialist. She thought he was an industrialist. She never quite understood his work. He had been to Harvard and Oxford. His mother was Viennese, his father American. He was born on Manhattan. One of the few. Most people arrive there. He had been born at home. At home on Park Avenue.

He seemed to be a banker, a lawyer, an industrialist. To Rosemary that simply meant he was rich. He never talked of his work. It was his decision. He had no desire to discuss his work. He was married with a family. A home on Fifth Avenue at Seventieth Street.

Rosemary would walk past his apartment within five minutes.

She would look up briefly. She would carry on walking.

A house in the country. A fleet of limousines, he took her abroad the entire time. Hotel suites in Paris, Rome, Geneva. The Connaught. They had first made love at the Plaza. Later he had given her a beautiful apartment on Central Park West and Sixty-Eighth Street. An area she now detested. The Upper West Side appalled her. From that apartment she was able to look over the park and see his building. That was wrong. When he was with her he wanted to make love. They made love. They made love well. They were well suited. He was tender. He was strong. He was very, very rich. They had fun together.

When she arrived in New York she was a painter. An artist. A fair one. She would never be great. But she was beautiful, intelligent and sensitive. She could use all these qualities in her painting. With her talent she could transfer these qualities to canvas.

She had been the assistant to a fashionable and highly thought of downtown painter. A man whose work hung at the best galleries. A new star. He had helped her. She had earned fair money. She lived. She had met many fascinating people. One of them was him. She met him at a SoHo party. That was not his usual territory. It was a happy coincidence. They had fallen in love. They had planned a date. Within a week they were lying in a king sized bed at the Plaza looking beyond the Park uptown and drinking champagne.

It was perfect. It lasted six years. It became painful. By the middle of the sixth year it was ugly. Last summer it had ended. She looked up and saw his apartment on Seventieth Street and Fifth Avenue. She looked straight ahead and continued walking. She had returned to London, her home city, for the remainder of that year, and to New York in January.

She was now hurrying. It was only in New York that she could exorcise the situation. It was now May. The sun was shining. Rosemary was no longer unhappy. It was a year since she had seen him. She had lost the apartment. She had painted at first, though hardly at all in those latter years. Her talent had certainly not developed. She had simply lived a full romantic life. Often she had hung around. Waiting for him. She hung around the wealthy. The successful. The parties. There was plenty of money in new York. Plenty. He had settled some money on her. She had a few possessions. A poor Impressionist. A good fur coat. She sold these things, keeping her jewellery. No mammoth amount. The jewels she owned were tasteful.

Renting a small apartment in the Village, she would have enough money to live for a while. She was not unhappy. It was simply that she had done nothing substantial with her life. She was bright, had intellect, reason. Rosemary had lived, loved, never really worked. She gave up her job with the painter shortly after the affair began. She was so often whisked away on jet planes. That was her destiny. She read a lot. She had always read. It was May; she was almost thirty, this was her life.

She looked up. It was the Metropolitan Museum. Time was her own. She was going to wander through the museum.

Inside the world of museums, of relics, Rosemary stopped and breathed. The air of museums. A similar air shared by cathedrals, religion and sphinxes.

It was the middle of the week, the middle of the afternoon. People came and went, as they do at museums. One might wait for everyone to assemble. They merely came and went.

Rosemary had no handbag. Unlike the European. No trappings. No trimmings. She had confused them to mean the same thing, and she accepted neither. Ever since she had been forced to sell her fur coat she had attempted to sell her past life with it. Without regret. It was a life she had chosen to lose. She now stood naked in her own freedom. She had no need of cloakrooms.

Walking toward the tombs, down marble corridors, past statues with stoney, broken noses, mosaic floors, patterns, shapes, uniformed attendants, she noticed nothing. Rosemary would not even bother to feign interest. She had come to the museum. Let that be enough.

The American wing. Early American Elegance. White House style. Reconstructed rooms. Turquoise. Buttercup yellow. Royal. All the same. All interiors. Rosemary had been to the White House, on a private tour. She had sat in the Blue Room.

On toward an Egyptian relic, colossal in size and bearing. An edifice of stone, transported from B.C. or was it A.D.? It was impressive. It existed. She inhaled Egyptian air. She parted the Red Sea. She looked out of endless glass windows at Manhattan sky and skyscrapers, overlooking little Egypt.

Walking on, along more corridors, feeling anxious, seeming to know someone was there, she turned around. Several people were following her; in that they were behind her; which happens in public; on streets and such. She continued. Observed. Watched. Wigman? European? Violinist? Karate? Industrialist? On she walked.

She arrived in a land of plants and fountains and Roman statuettes. Surrounded by glass. The sound of trickling water. She sat by the mild tepid fountain, on a low stone wall. She had encountered much stone that day. Then one did in Manhattan. It is built on stone.

Suddenly she craned her neck with a strong angular movement and her eyes met another's. A woman who was positively staring at her. Rosemary stared back. The woman was not beautiful, yet stunning, effective. She was short. Not petite. And she wore no heels. Sneakers, beige army pants, a mass of short, well-cut curls, dark brown, a curved Roman nose. She was utterly striking. She wore expensive sunglasses, though Rosemary knew she was staring and it did not unnerve her. It caused her to quiver. The woman stared deliberately. Rosemary with equal deliberation, walked up to the woman.

"I seem to interest you."

"No, you fascinate me."

At the woman's suggestion they went for coffee. Another fountain, a lake, more statues, Art Nouveau, a table by the water.

The woman, Alexandra, was from Argentina. They sat sipping coffee. An Englishwoman and an Argentinian woman. Sipping coffee by the man-made lake in the Metropolitan Museum, in New York City, in the middle of the week in May.

Rosemary's anxiety had turned to thrilling confusion. She had slept with no-one since last summer. She had slept with no-one else in those six years. She had slept with no woman. No, never. Suddenly, this summer, she knew she was sitting opposite a woman who wanted her. A woman who would not give her up.

That afternoon in the museum Alexandra and Rosemary became inseparable. That was what Alexandra wanted. But Rosemary was a strong woman. She had taken the woman's telephone number when offered and left. Rosemary was not going to give out her telephone number. Not to a positive stranger. She had walked home. All the way downtown. She was strong. She was fit. She was actually unnerved. In a state of panic. She knew she was no longer alone.

She made a sandwich. She ate a morsel. She got into bed. She tried to read. She tried to watch television. All was useless. She was distracted. She had given six years. She had loved him passionately. She was an extraordinary, unselfish lover. She deserved to be a wife. That was what she had really wanted, she thought.

Breathing Argentinian air, she was fighting fit. She lay on her bed and clutching her ankles she cried into the night.

Rosemary was woken the next day by the telephone. She felt full of sleep, her eyes crusted, her face ironed out by rest. However, a ringing telephone is a persistent animal.

Alexandra was somehow suddenly saying hello to Rosemary. She was arranging a breakfast meeting, in the Village, in an adorable café near Rosemary's apartment. Rosemary questioned nothing, merely agreed the arrangement that Alexandra was making; followed instructions.

She ran a bath and stretched her limbs. She was wanted, by a woman. Did that suit her? Did it matter? It was human contact, care, possible love. She would live again. That mattered.

She dried and dressed, locked her door, and with a carefree spirit that anyone might have envied, she strode, that sunny May morning, towards brioche and fun.

The two women sat opposite each other, Alexandra's bare foot running over Rosemary's shoe. Sipping orange juice. With bird-like appetites they scanned the pancakes, french toast, syrup, bacon, endless eggs, marmalades, waffles, bagels and meagrely, almost shyly, ordered croissant and a bowl of strawberries. And coffee. Lots of strong, fresh, black coffee.

"What shall we do today?"

Rosemary was shocked. How bold this woman was. Did she really consider that she had claim to Rosemary's entire day? Breakfast had been the only arrangement. She did not think she had misled this woman. She had made no further plans. There were other things she ought to get on with that day. She could not simply lose all routine. She could not afford to give way to heady impulses. Next this woman would be claiming Rosemary for the entire weekend!

"I'm all yours," were the words Rosemary discovered slipping from her mouth.

Oh, such weakness. Such wicked weakness. If she started in this manner the entire adventure was destined for doom, doom and failure. She must hang onto her reason. She had trained this reason of hers. She must not forego it now.

By the time Rosemary had been able to gather all these reasonable thoughts together, the two women were giggling and chuckling like old schoolfriends. Like two convent girls departing from London, one who now lived in Paris, the other in Tokyo, meeting after so long in another major city, foreigners together. So familiar, so caring, so understanding.

Coffee after coffee was consumed. Topic upon topic dismissed. They were friends. They were happy. Rosemary certainly was happy. She was breathing, and so easily. She was not even aware of breathing. It just happened.

They walked into the street. Into the sun. They had known each other for twenty hours. Pain, it occurred to Rosemary, must be faced alone. Pleasure would always find its fellows. You can never experience pleasure alone. True pleasure. There will always be someone at your side for those moments of pleasure.

Rosemary found herself walking side by side with the Argentinian woman. Life had introduced them and mutual pleasure brought them together. Rosemary was determined not to allow her past to separate them. Her past was behind her, a matter of small consequence. The present seemed to be taking care of itself. The future was something out of her range. Out of her present concern.

She and Alexandra walked across to the Hudson then down to Battery Park. Occasionally Alexandra might take Rosemary's hand in hers, put her arm around Rosemary's shoulders, she was tender, she was kind. She was concerned and gentle. Considerate and generous. Qualities one sought in a companion.

Alexandra had been married, twice, had had numerous lovers, male and female, and now, at the age of thirty-eight, had realised it was women she adored. Women she understood and misunderstood in the correct way, women she needed. The only thing she used to miss about men was that silly and often disappointing promontory. Now, she had overcome this and women alone alone held the real charm.

Much of this was extraordinary to Rosemary, occasionally appalling. After all, that 'promontory' had been a great deal of Rosemary's lifeline. It had meant a lot to her, nevertheless she was fascinated and Alexandra made her laugh.

Sometimes, slyly, Alexandra would steal at Rosemary's neck puckishly with her two strong rosy lips. It caused Rosemary to shudder, she enjoyed it so.

They spent the afternoon at the World Trade Centre, they observed the city, they laughed and chattered relentlessly. In the evening they went to the movies. Alexandra frequently leaned across and took Rosemary's hand during the film. She stroked her leg. Behaved in a most relaxed manner as if she were Rosemary's lover. Rosemary was no longer interested in reason; she was going to allow everything that was happening to happen.

After the cinema they ate, quietly, peacefully, gazing across the restaurant table at one another. Then after dinner, at Rosemary's suggestion, they went for a long walk, downtown. A walk which ended at Rosemary's front door. Rosemary leaned over and for the first time placed a gentle peck upon Alexandra's cheek. She thanked her for a lovely day and disappeared into her apartment.

Alexandra, a little stunned, knew that was the way it was. Certainly for that night.

The moments of bliss they continued to share ran into hours of happiness. To days of utter content. Walking together. Eating ice-creams. Going to movies, art galleries. Even to the beach. They shared everything. Everything except for that remaining unresolved issue: The Heart Of The Night. That was spent alone.

Each morning the telephone rang and awoke Rosemary in her own apartment. And each morning her heart leapt as she realised the Argentinian was still on the line. Still hooked.

It was no game that Rosemary played. It was no case of tantalising torturing. It was her fear witholding her. Her reason which intervened. She could not, she contemplated, go further. Despite all this joy, all this terror, all this internal passion, Rosemary still had her reason. Rosemary was persistently a reasonable woman. She was happy to be loved. She loved the attention she received. She doted on this care. She returned such emotions with similar generosity.

Alexandra by now, was falling quite rapidly, quite fully, in love with Rosemary. That love gave her patience. The patience to wait for Rosemary's added attention. She would wait for that thing which ultimately would be worth waiting for, worth having.

Then one particular morning the telephone rang in a different way, with a new urgency. It alarmed Rosemary. It made her bolt upright in her downied bed. It made her aware of the real morning sooner than she had expected. She now expected someone else to be on the other end of the telephone line. A person she did not care to hear from. But no, it was Alexandra. There was no difference. They made their arrangements. It had been Rosemary's imagination. Nothing had changed. Alexandra was constant.

Today was their ninth day together. Nine had always been Rosemary's lucky number, it was probably this that had made her too sensitive. There was always the chance that luck would run out. She was over-reacting.

They met in Central Park. It was 11 a.m. and already eighty-two degrees. They walked around the park hand in hand for more than an hour. Alexandra announced that she should take Rosemary to the Four Seasons for lunch. They would drink champagne and celebrate their union. It was as if, it occurred to Rosemary, Alexandra knew it was Day Nine. They sat in the chic restaurant, sipping champagne, eating lightly, daintily.

In the afternoon they sailed the Circle Line Boat. Two tourists. Touring life together, right around the city, in burning late May heat. Sipping soda water and sweating. Wearing sun shades and burning. Rosemary had no hat. She didn't care. Let her skin brown. Let it roast. She was alive and touching the elements. She would allow them to touch her.

Later that evening having smoked a pure grass joint, she found herself in Alexandra's bed, high up over the city, the world, on Madison and Seventy Eigth, lying low, drowning in the bed, lying naked.

In the late evening when the darkness had barely touched the room to its full extent, cuddled in each other's care, concerned with one another's being, entwined in their mutual respect and ecstasy, the two women fell asleep to dream.

The next morning, Rosemary found herself walking across Seventy Eight street toward the park. It was 8 a.m. and no ringing telephone had brought her into this day. She had left the sleeping Alexandra deep in her dreams, had quietly dressed and was walking home.

Alexandra had a gun in her apartment. For all her independence she kept a gun. To ward off ominous offenders? The gun had shocked Rosemary, had jolted her. It was sitting in the hall on a table. The table where Rosemary had left a little purse. She had, since knowing Alexandra, started carrying handbags once more. She could cope with the ordinary. It no longer offended her.

When she left that morning she had pondered over the gun. Paid it too much attention. Now she had arrived at Fifth Avenue. Instead of walking ahead and straight into the park she turned left, downtown. She was walking alone on Fifth Avenue as she had been those ten days ago, only now travelling in the opposite direction. It was the first time she had walked alone since meeting Alexandra. She was alone and she had the courage to walk alone. And what is more, Rosemary knew exactly where she was going.

At 8.30 a.m. precisely she was on Fifth Avenue at Seventieth Street. Opposite was the apartment building where the Industrialist lived. Outside the building was his limousine and chauffeur who took him to his office every morning at 8.45 a.m. Every morning at 9 a.m. he sat behind his desk. The hard working, zealous executive.

Thanks to Alexandra, Rosemary now had the courage, and the knowledge. She would do this for women everywhere. She had deserved more. She had deserved not to be used, to be jilted. She could have been a wife. She deserved true love. Men could not behave in such a fashion. With such callousness.

For fifteen minutes she patiently waited. At 8.45 a.m. she crossed over Fifth Avenue. He came out of the building, she called his name. He looked at her. Puzzled, then anxious. He seemed concerned to ignore her. Rosemary pulled Alexandra's gun from her purse, and with pride and nervousness, with the same wicked fear that had made her pick up the gun that morning, she pointed it towards his heart and shot. He hit the stone of the sidewalk and lay in a pool of blood.

She waited for the doorman or the chauffeur or the passers-by, to leave him in his drowning blood and approach her. To call for help. To call for law and order. And while she waited she felt she was right in what she had done. It had been what she had wanted and now she would be able to face her life, knowing for her, life could only be tomorrow and tomorrow.

· · · · ·

PART TWO

The black limousine arrived at the building at quarter to nine. The driver remained inside. At nine o'clock exactly Anne-Marie stepped out of her apartment building. The one that was once theirs.

She was mesmerically thin. Dressed in a superbly cut black suit which accentuated her thinness. Mourning became her. She walked, without a glance to left or right, toward the limousine, the driver now holding the door open. Trailing behind her a boy and girl, the one under the age of ten, the other just over. Anne-Marie stepped confidently but quietly into the car. The children followed. The door was shut. The driver resumed his place. They glided silently away. She had been a widow, she thought, for four days. It had been four days since his murder. Her husband. An Industrialist, Banker, Lawyer. No criminal had been brought to justice. No witness had arrived with any helpful information. A cruel, clueless act of some crank.

Anne-Marie had led an idyllic existence, one which escaped any scandal. Two beautiful children, endless parties, two gorgeous homes. Gorgeous was the fitting word. They travelled abroad together, and although he made occasional trips on business without her, he always returned with some exquisite small jewel.

She had charge accounts at Saks, Bonwit-Teller and Bloomingdales; she had learned to cook, doted on the children, never tired of reading to them. Never tired of reading to herself. She tackled Flaubert, Balzac, occasionally Dickens and of course Austen. The Brontës she found a little too gloomy in not quite the right way. She had a season ticket for the Met. and was always there to boo the poor Macbeths and cheer the great Aidas. She visited all the serious new plays on Broadway and even had a best friend who voted for the Tony awardees. She always made clear her opinion of the season to this friend who took great notice.

She often ate lunch at the Four Seasons where she would discuss works of charity with fellow good-deeders. Regularly took the children to the movies, a five o'clock show, they saw all the films of Spielberg again and again, and to follow always a burger and shakes.

Once a week she threw a lavish and well-ordered dinner party; canapés accompanied by perfectly chilled glasses of vintage Bollinger, business associates of her husband with their wives, a few celebrities and always someone from the art world.

Anne-Marie adored modern art, secretly she longed to be a painter.

An immaculate dinner around the sixteenth century refectory table. Expertly blended coffee with liqueurs and Godiva chocolates taken in the drawing room around the B movie fire – a contraption operated by gas but purporting to be fuelled by hand chopped logs.

Once a month an even larger party for around three dozen or two score; delicious salmon served with all manner of ice-cold vegetables. At weekends, a large house opened its New England doors to them, and the children would play ball in its spacious gardens, frolic in its pool, ride ponies in its paddocks.

Anne-Marie would cook and freeze and watch t.v. and read. They also made love there. They made love well there. He was relaxed. He would play with the children and make love with her. Although he did not arrive until Saturday night right before supper he would leave all apparent cares behind. It was another world, a world of pastel shades and delicate chintz prints, Italian tiled bathrooms and freshness all about them. Fresh air. Mondays back to Fifth Avenue and their penthouse overlooking Central Park.

And now, Anne-Marie thought to herself, he was gone, lost to her, her children, and the world.

She sat in the back of the limousine, self-contained, superb in black, a child to either side on her way to his cremation. In a word Anne-Marie was *chic*.

The crematorium was situated on the Upper West Side. A fitting place, it occurred to Anne-Marie, to return to ash.

It was nine twenty when the car pulled up outside the vast, gloomy, castle-like doors of the emporium. By ten fifteen she was safely restored to the comfort of her black limousine. The service had been brief, well attended, suitably sermoned and now, thank God, was over.

She wondered about the stranger in headscarf and dark glasses she had noticed weeping silently as she left the crematorium. "Some crank . . . " she thought dismissively.

The car moved away.

The children had gone in another car with their nanny, in another direction. Probably to the zoo. Hot fudge sundaes at Serendipity. Diversions.

Guy Richards, who was sitting alongside Anne-Marie, reached across and pressed her hand in a comforting little squeeze. She looked up and smiled at Guy, then with no danger of causing offence, withdrew her hand, reached into her purse, and lit a St. Moritz cigarette.

Guy, who was more than extremely handsome, and no more than thirty-five, was a close, even intimate associate of her husband. Or rather he *had* been. Her husband had referred to him as Dickie claiming that to be the diminitive of Richards, though this made little sense to Anne-Marie. Guy was one of Manhattan's most eligible bachelors. Athletic, intelligent, rich and successful, and easy going, humorous.

Outside of his beautifully tailored business suits his dress sense was 'preppy'. Pastel sportshirts with emblems on their left breast. Khaki pants handsomely cut to flatter the behind. Navy blue or bottle green deck shoes. A fine and masculine watch.

"So..." Guy had started talking, softly but firmly. He discussed wills, stocks, shares, trusts, the children's education, her apartment, the business, her home in the country, her friends, her new life. Anne-Marie paid little or no attention. Her mind was wandering. She was bored, bored of all this. She announced that she was feeling tired, they would have to skip brunch. Certainly for that day. She was after all a widow.

The journey continued in silence, while Anne-Marie decided, quite definitely, there and then, that widowhood was a state that simply did not suit her. What Anne-Marie knew she needed was an adventure, a trip, an escapade to allow her to feel something, anything but the pangs of solitary widowhood.

The limousine glided to a perfect halt and both Guy and the chauffeur were suddenly opening doors and guiding her toward the lobby.

Before swinging through the circular doors with that swish of chic, which came so easily to her, she kissed Guy in the European fashion, thanked him for his support and loyalty and before Guy could be discreet, chivalrous, loyal and supportive she was gone.

Inside the apartment all was quiet.

No maids. No window washers. No sherry-reception post-cremation. No children. Simply quiet. She flung off her heels, slipped out of her black Dior, pulled on a pristine white ankle length bath robe, poured herself a vodka, perched on a ledge in a window and gazed at the green park, at the city's summer.

She wondered what her husband made of Guy. Maybe they had had an affair! She laughed, her husband had been far too solid a man to have had an affair with anyone. Far too faithful. Far, in fact, too busy.

She looked down at her elegantly draped legs and wondered if Guy had time for affairs, and whose time he was sharing. He always stayed in town at weekends and never dated the same girl on more than two or three occasions.

On a whim Anne-Marie jumped down from her ledge, devoured the remaining vodka, reached for a Yellow Pages, push-dialled her telephone and ordered a Hertz-Rent-A-Car. "One week, possibly two, possibly longer still," were the requirements of the Chic Widow. "No. I'll collect it myself this afternoon."

That afternoon as Anne-Marie sat behind the steering wheel of her Stratos Blue Ford Mustang, smoking a St. Moritz, she acknowledged a small pang of pride within her. Pride in her actions. She was, after all, most newly widowed. And here she was sailing gaily through green light upon green light in a car no-one would recognise, travelling way downtown to Battery Park to sit and gaze at the Statue of Liberty. She flipped open the glove compartment. Inside was a tape, left no doubt by the previous driver. She pressed the tape firmly into the cassette socket and out blasted the terribly New York tones of Bruce Springsteen.

She arrived at Battery Park and found a parking space. She got out of the car and was horrified to be amongst hordes of tourists alighting and embarking the stream of boats that carried them across to the Liberty Lady and back.

She entered an area bordering the water and secured a place on a bench. She contemplated visiting Guy at his Murray Hill apartment. She contemplated following him.

Her thoughts were broken as a passing shadow deprived her of sunlight. Looking up she saw the same young woman who had wept that morning at her husband's cremation. Anne-Marie was forced to stare, but the young woman did not seem to notice her, did not seem to care.

Her attentions were transfixed on a vagabond, a silly man in an old mac wearing a ridiculous wig, in endless conversation with himself and anyone who might pass by. Occasionally he would direct an exclusive remark to the young woman, who embraced such moments and laughed lightly, pleasantly. Although they did not seem to be together, they had a shorthand, a relationship.

"How uncanny," thought Anne-Marie. "How peculiar." It *was* peculiar that this woman should have that day entered her real life and now, already, have made this slight intrusion on her secret life.

Anne-Marie moved on. She wanted nothing to do with this female or her comrade-vagrant in his wig. This, most assuredly, was not part of her plan.

She did not know whether to search for another place on another bench. She decided to leave. Her mind was empty. Aching to start her adventure she could concentrate on nothing for any length of time. As soon as a thought arrived in her conscious mind another followed. Mostly to do with her life. His death. The future. She was able to work out nothing. She got back into her Stratos Blue Ford Mustang and with a sense of urgency drove uptown. The remainder of the afternoon was to be spent at the movies. Alone. Without popcorn. That was where she wanted to be until she went home. Home to face the remainder of her life. To spend time with her children.

And after the movie, having parked the car in a pay-garage not far from her apartment, she walked slowly home to do just that.

During the days that followed, Anne-Marie reverted to her maternal role. She was a little fragile, certainly, but that was only too normal in such circumstances. She amused her children, read to them, cooked them their suppers, bathed them and allowed them to watch too much television.

By the weekend she had sent them off, on a train, to their maternal grandmother's house, one hour away in the country. She told the servants to take the weekend off. She wanted to be alone. In this Garboesque state Anne-Marie prepared to face her first period of widowhood. Alone.

That Friday evening, at nine o'clock, Anne-Marie left behind the splendour of her Manhattan apartment, with its glorious vistas of Central Park, and walked to the nearby pay-garage where her secret Ford Mustang lay waiting. It was a beautiful evening, not too balmy, allowing one to breathe easily. She wore denim jeans, pumps and a light sweatshirt. Casual. Bruce accompanied her on the journey. Chanting his various tales. Anne-Marie observed the walking city from her Mustang; the last of the day's shoppers, the first of the night's adventurers. None of them really concerned Anne-Marie. She was a secret person. Separate. She drove downtown to Murray Hill where Guy Richards had an apartment.

She arrived at Lexington and Thirtieth Street and parked her car right across from Guy's building. A perfect view. Directly opposite. Bruce sang and Anne-Marie waited. For fifteen minutes she waited, for twenty, thirty, an hour. She played side one, side two, side one, the radio. She watched the passers-by passing by, pass by and not notice her, no-one she knew. She watched people coming and going from the building where she had hoped to see Guy come and go, and then, before she knew where she was, what she had been thinking, what time of night it now was, how many cigarettes she had smoked, or what she was feeling, he ventured forth.

Guy Richards left the apartment building where he lived and was on the street. Not so very strange. It was after all the weekend. He did have a right to be in such a place. He wore khaki pants, topsiders, a sportshirt. He looked handsome and clean. Fresh and ready. For what she wondered? But she was not to wonder for long. Guy opened the door of *his* Stratos Blue Ford and got in. He was a slow and careful driver, Anne-Marie was easily able to follow him. He drove downtown staying on the Lower East Side until he entered a garage on East Fourth Street. A garage not unlike the one Anne-Marie had used to house *her* Stratos Blue Ford. A few minutes after Guy and his car disappeared Anne-Marie approached the garage. She was refused entry because she did not hold the correct plastic card. Flummoxed but not phased Anne-Marie politely enquired as to the whereabouts of the exit of this garage.

"Back of the block," were the words she received.

A swift drive around the block and with suitable dexterity she parked her Stratos Blue Ford in a perfectly sized space directly opposite the exit. She checked her watch, 11.30 p.m. She waited.

For fiteen minutes Anne-Marie waited. Patiently. Then thirty minutes passed and she began to tire of Bruce, of the radio, of smoking. It was now past midnight and Anne-Marie was beginning to become altogether tired of waiting for Guy Richards and his Stratos Blue Ford to appear.

Still she waited. Cars left the garage. Bikes. A few pedestrians. But nowhere Guy. "Damn!" thought Anne-Marie.

"Capital damn, damn, damn!"

At one o'clock in the morning she drove uptown, parked her car in its hiding place and walked with a certain fatigue back to her glorious apartment.

She slept well that night. The past week had been a strenuous time. A lot had happened to alter Anne-Marie's life.

Unimpressed by her dreams she awoke the next morning with restored energy. She did not appear concerned with the facts relating to her husband's recent death. His murder. Her widowhood. Her apparent lack of grieving. She knew inside she was fighting a chaos but she had her own way of dealing with it. Her own method.

She squeezed some oranges, drank some coffee, ate some lightly buttered toast. It felt strange to wake and be alone. Alone in life. To have no-one to care for. No demands to be met. But for this day, and possibly this day only, Anne-Marie was alone. Alone and free. It was a day which passed quickly, without incident. By nine thirty, nine forty-five that evening, Anne-Marie was parked opposite the apartment building where Guy Richards lived, smoking a cigarette and thumbing through the complete works of Bruce Springsteen, purchased by her earlier that day.

Time passed. But this time Anne-Marie was ready. Prepared to wait. She guessed it unlikely that Guy would appear before eleven or so. This knowledge gave her patience. She had only arrived early in case she might miss him. But her knowledge of Guy told her he was a man of habit. A constant creature.

Looking like a man about to take his dog on a late night stroll,

Guy left his building at 11.15 p.m. Only there was no dog.

She followed Guy to the same garage, watched the Stratos Blue Ford disappear up the ramps, then drove rapidly around the block to the exit. She was determined this time not to lose Mr. Richards.

She waited but Guy did not appear. She did not think he was still inside but he had not left in his car. So, he must be leaving the garage by means of a different exit. Or of course by means of a different car! How could she have been so slow? Then again hadn't she closely scrutinised every driver that left the garage? "Damn!" blasted out Anne-Marie. A damn that spent too much of her precious little energy. With Bruce quite wound down and another pack of St Moritz gone, Anne-Marie fell asleep.

She awoke with a crick in her neck, feeling quite unrested, the sound of a nearby honking horn to remind her where she was and no Manhattan birdsong, though it was dawn.

"Damn!" she thought "I must have fallen asleep." Now awake, a tiny throaty cough, she started up the engine and prepared to move off. Almost simultaneously, and almost escaping her notice, Guy Richards pulled out of the garage exit in his Ford and drove off. Anne-Marie's heart leapt. Her stomach rose up. She was suddenly nervous, tired and hungry. She followed Guy in his car right the way to the door of his apartment building. He parked, got out and donning a pair of shades entered the building, saying goodnight to the Sunday morn.

There! She had always had an inkling about Guy Richards. Now she had spied him hanging about in car parks in the middle of the night. The car park was obviously a front for some illicit den, some desperate haunt, some iniquitous celebration . . .

Anne-Marie felt elated. Like one who has received glowing marks for homework. She dashed home, made a cup of chocolate malt and fell asleep. Later that morning the alarm rang. She immediately phoned Guy to ask him to join her for brunch. "That will throw him."

But she was unable to speak with Guy, his answering service picked up the telephone asking if they might take any message.

"Yes," said Anne-Marie, "ask Mr. Richards to call Anne-Marie please. Urgent."

Guessing he would not waken before twelve or one and knowing the service would report the exact time she had called, she hoped to catch him off his guard allowing her to ask all manner of questions.

By 2.30 p.m. Guy had not returned her call and Anne-Marie had decided that it would be quite wrong to ask any questions of him or to attempt to arrange a meeting in the hope of catching him out. She would simply have to wait one more week, until next Friday when she would again be free to follow him. Next Friday the children could go off visiting again. Next Friday she felt sure Guy would go visiting again. Next time she would find a way into that garage. She would get even closer to Mr. Richards and what made him tick.

The telephone rang. It was 3.15 p.m.

"Hello Guy. No, I was only calling because I wondered if you felt like having brunch with me today. Too late now. Never mind . . . Oh, you played squash early and then had brunch in the village . . .?"

Then Guy was onto the children, papers to sign and blah, blah, blah. There! She had caught him red-handed. Well almost. He couldn't have gone to bed at six and played squash at ten. Only badly. Anyway she knew he hadn't.

"Yes, well, this week's not right for me Guy. Give me a little longer."

Goodbyes were said and Anne-Marie slipped into a chic but comforting grey cotton dress. In an hour or two the children would return and she would be once more Mother and Widow.

At five o'clock that afternoon Anne-Marie jumped into a taxi-cab and went to Grand Central Station to meet her children. At the station she crossed to the giant arrivals board to see when their train would be in. Finding the correct listing for Wilton, Connecticut, their grandmother's home, she noted the appropriate platform.

Walking towards platform 9, avoiding the milling crowds, she glimpsed a young woman lolling against a news-stand eating potato chips. Anne-Marie continued towards her platform. Feeling chilly, goose-pimples racing down her spine, Anne-Marie pulled her cashmere scarf closely around her. She looked back at the news-stand and although she could not be sure, she thought she recognised the woman.

Arriving at platform 9, she watched the train pulling into its bay. She looked back a second time to the news-stand, the stranger had moved. She was walking away from Anne-Marie across the vast lobby of Grand Central Station. Anne-Marie bristled as she realised it was the same young woman she had encountered at her husband's cremation, the same person at Battery Park . . . The clattering of carriage doors broke nearby and Anne-Marie was caught in the comforting embrace of her excited children.

"Burgers and shakes?"

"Yes, yes, yes!"

It was with great anticipation and a little trepidation, that Anne-Marie awoke the following Friday. The past week had been a trial, she had felt miserable, misplaced, lonely, had snapped at the children, suffered a growing loss of identity and often couldn't shift from her armchair, an unread book lying open upon her unloved lap.

It was thrilling to be able to leave behind the real, the ordinary person she was and venture back into her land of the unknown. The children would go directly from school to their grandmother's house, accompanied by their nanny. The rest of the servants were once again given the weekend off. The cook had prepared sufficient food, the windows were washed, the bills paid. Anne-Marie had nothing to sign, no-one to see. It was surprising, to realise how few friends she really had. How little the people around her seemed to care. She supposed that most of the people she knew were met through her husband. She was not a woman in need of constant companionship. She was not a woman given to the Lunching-With-Girlfriends syndrome. She found herself alone.

At eleven o'clock that Friday night, having drunk two large

vodkas, having driven downtown with Bruce, having parked her Stratos Blue Ford Mustang bang opposite the exit to Mr. Richards' downtown hideaway, Anne-Marie in headscarf and rose tinted shades was standing bang opposite the entrance to that very same building.

And sure enough, twenty minutes later, up pulled Guy Richards in his Stratos Blue Ford. Flashing his piece of plastic he entered the forbidden territory. That place, that cavern that Anne-Marie so desperately, though she knew not why, longed to enter.

As quick as lightning she circled the block and arrived at the exit. She knew she would have to wait for someone to come out as the door only pushed in one direction. The direction toward Anne-Marie. For seven minutes she waited. Patiently. Then, in a moment of pique, as the word *damn* was about to explode from her mouth, the door pushed open and a most ordinary middle-aged couple left the building.

"Damn!" yelled Anne-Marie. "I've left my purse in the car." And a most obliging middle-aged man, be-hatted about his head and be-chequered about his body, held open the exit door, allowing Anne-Marie into her wonderland.

She was inside. Quiet. No. The sound of distant voices. The silent roar of an expensive engine. Concrete. Strip lights. A garage. She had entered on the ground floor where there were not many parked cars. Above her four more floors, below her one. The basement. Instinct or madness had led her this far, she was determined to pursue her feelings.

After glancing through the Fords, Chevys and Chryslers she went nervously down the stairway to the basement. What if she bumped into Guy? What would she say? What lie could she tell? Voices approaching. The voices of men. She gripped the dirty metal side-rail and stood still, frozen on the concrete steps. Aggresive male voices. Rapists? Two young men in denims with kindly faces passed her by on the stairs and headed toward the exit. She needed to call upon those resources of cool which guided her through so many situations in life. She pulled herself together and gathered her strength from the tip of her toes upwards. She was doing nothing wrong. She regained her composure, her will, her curiosity, she became once again nervous in the correct way, a little high, a sense of danger. She continued.

Entering the basement of the garage, a considerably smaller space than the ground floor, she spied, almost immediately, the Stratos Blue Ford belonging to Guy. There was no orgy, no feast of drug addiction, boozing or sexual misbehaviour, just a few more cars innocently awaiting their keepers, and, alongside Guy's car a beautiful motor-cycle, gleaming in black and silver. A shining example of modern technology a large machine, aggressive and macho with its own sexual innuendo.

Spotting a head bobbing up and down in Guy's car she sidestepped silently behind a concrete pillar. She peered out, in the back seat of the car was a body contorting itself into unusual angles. There! She knew it. Guy Richards frequented pay garages for the purpose of having sex on back seats each weekend around midnight.

Wait!

Supposing it wasn't sex that Guy was involved in? Supposing it were violence? He may be murdering man, woman, teenager, child, even now!

With her fiery imagination pursuing such lines of thought, Anne-Marie stared at the Ford for five whole minutes. It's door flew open. Anne-Marie's lower lip dropped several inches leaving her mouth in an ugly gaping position. Guy Richards was standing dressed from head to toe in black leather. On his feet a handsome and sturdy pair of black leather biker's boots with fine strong silver buckles on the side. A pair of beautifully cut black leather pants clung to his legs, his crotch, his thighs, his waist. A black string vest about his chest, and over this a jacket, again in black leather, but unlike the pants beaten and old. His blonde hair, tousled atop his head, was run through with a little grease. His bones more sunken than ever. His eyes deeper set. He looked like a movie star and as she watched she realised she was touching her own breast, holding herself. Guy Richards, for whom she felt a certain contempt, a definite mocking, was, in this clandestine world, a most desirable member of the male species.

Anne-Marie wanted to rush across the basement and throw her body over the motor-cycle, sink her teeth into his leather pants, devour his crotch through that leather with her perfectly whitened teeth. She craved his flesh.

Guy, unaware of his effect was still getting into character, preparing for the role he was to play for the remainder of the night. Locking the door of his Stratos Blue Ford containing his khaki pants, bottle green topsiders, Lacoste shirt. Anne-Marie guessed that Guy was about to leave the garage upon that motor cycle. Silently leaving her pillar she retraced her steps to her own car ready to follow this creature on his bike, wherever he might lead her.

This was not what she had expected, erotic feelings. She had been the most perfect of wives, the most monogamous, had enjoyed the most enviable of sex lives.

Before she could allow herself another thought, the handsome roar of the motor cycle spoke to her and frantically lighting cigarettes and ejecting Bruce and casting aside rose tinted shades, Anne-Marie found herself in hot pursuit. Of what, she could not know. But, unlike her poor dear husband, she felt most alive.

Guy crossed town on his shining cycle and Anne-Marie followed as best she could, knowing it would be difficult to follow a motor-cycle if it sped away at green lights. But Guy drove his machine like a sane person, not a maniac so she was able to keep up.

He pulled over on the Lower West Side not far from the Hudson River, parked his bike and entered a bar called Riders.

Anne-Marie desperately wanted to enter the bar but knew she must be content to wait for Guy to reappear. Besides she had a hunch that Guy was not stopping at Riders for the rest of Friday night, but merely passing through.

She had brought a small flask of vodka with her and now seemed the moment to fortify herself. She gulped greedily at the spirit. A mixture of nerves and anticipation made her behave coarsely.

She watched the night's prowlers, in their denim and leather, cruise by and check her out. It was a lively neighbourhood. A block further back there had been bookshops and leather stores next to grocery stores and chocolate shops. A predominantly male neighbourhood. Just as it had been the day of her husband's cremation. Maybe some of these men were other workmates of her husband. These males.

Thinking of the crematorium Anne-Marie recalled the mysterious weeping woman. Who was she? Had she known her husband? Known something of his death?

The door of Riders swung open and a black figure strolled provocatively towards Guy's motor cycle. Throwing a leg over the machine with a certain thrust he started the engine and roared off.

It struck Anne-Marie, as she frantically chased the cycle, how much more agressive Guy was after a few beers. This time she didn't follow him for long just a few blocks. He pulled across the main highway and stopped his bike in a large, deserted yard in front of a derelict warehouse backing onto the Hudson River. He kicked his leg over the bike and strode, western-style, toward the abandoned building.

She had expected him to go to some exotic party, or at very least to venture into Central Park. But this, this wandering off on some solitary stroll in romantic mood alongside the river. What should she now do?

She waited a few moments until Guy had disappeared into some blackness. Then she swung her car into the yard and pulled up as close as she dare to the building. She did not feel inclined to get out and walk into such a deserted place. What should she do? As she was about to dip her headlights and take some breathing space to consider her next move the strong lamps of her car revealed other characters entering the warehouse where she had imagined Guy in pleasant isolation. She dipped her lights and in the space of five minutes she witnessed ten, twelve, thirteen men come and go. Enter and leave.

She felt an urge to jump out of her Stratos Blue Ford, abandon all *bourgeoisiement* and rush toward this secret port of call.

This was something she dared not do.

She swung her car almost full circle and raising the dust of the yard sky high, she sped toward the relief and safety of Manhattan's lights.

Anne-Marie awoke the following morning pleasantly stirred by the memory of her erotic dreams. With new energy she made coffee, bathed herself and left her home. She collected her secret automobile and drove downtown to the exact location she had visited the night before. She pulled into a car park, a block away from Guy's warehouse haunt alongside the Hudson. She lit a St. Moritz and slammed the door.

She descended the piss-stained stairway to the fiercely trafficked street. Not a part of town she had much visited. This startlingly anonymous land of derelict edifices where lone dark figures wandered at all times of day and dirty night. She crossed the angry car fumes and with a knowing smile she passed a particular bar named Riders. She walked toward the heart of Christopher Street. To one of the leather stores she had noticed last night.

At first she felt foolish and lacked the spirit to go in. She wandered past once, twice, three times. She contemplated turning back. Returning the car to Hertz. Reverting to her roles of Mother and Widow. Some madness had propelled her to this point, she felt she must continue.

Browsing through the leather store Anne-Marie was amazed at the large selection of cock-rings and other sexual paraphanalia. She had never been to such an establishment heterosexual or otherwise. Now, in this otherwise place, she carefully selected black leather pants, biker's jacket, peaked cap, construction boots, white vests.

"Shopping for your little brother?" was the cute observation of the moustachioed, plaid-shirted, sales-assistant. Paying with crisp dollar bills then firmly gripping her flimsy, brown paper sack, she left.

As a man might buy underwear for a wife, a mistress, or even himself, she too had entered forbidden territory and taken a bite into the Big Apple. She drove quietly, calmly, uptown, a St. Moritz fuming in one hand, Mozart replacing Springsteen on the radio.

Parking the car in the pay-garage, locking the purchases in the trunk, Anne-Marie walked slowly across to her favourite store. Bloomingdales.

Safely behind her, in a hidden drawer, in a concrete garage, sat the costume of a character she would soon assume. Now however, for this moment in time, she needed to play at being Anne-Marie again. If only for a few hours. She chose to spend the remainder of the afternoon as she might on any regular Saturday.

That evening, having played the role of Anne-Marie for a suitably worthwhile period, having returned to the garage to unload her leather goods, having gulped a generous measure of vodka, she found herself in her well-lit bathroom, gazing at her male self in the full length mirror. The perfectly fitting leather trousers, the discarded string vest which revealed too much breast replaced by a brush cotton one, the face scrubbed of all make-up, the hair gelled into a suitable chaos, she stared harshly at that reflected self, contemplating how she appeared to be almost the real thing. Hiking on her boots, pulling on her jacket, slipping the black leather peaked cap into its top position she felt ready for another vodka.

She strode through her apartment to the ever so apt sounds of Lou Reed and gulped another vodka. She pranced in front of her mirror, gyrated, posed, was generally erotic. She began to feel sensual. Almost horny. Close to masturbation. She took another vodka. Her last, she decided, for the time being. She lit a cigarette. Her inner-self was adopting a most masculine manner. Gone was the chic widow. Gone were the weeds. She was in black certainly, but not in mourning for herself.

Checking her watch – ten o'clock – she realised she should remove all jewellery, that tiny gold chain about her neck, her rings. No perfume, no tantalising extras.

She filled a hip flask with chilled vodka. She locked her

apartment, pulled the peak of her cap to shade her eyes and upper face, descended in the elevator and walked directly past the doorman without either of them batting an eyelid. He had not recognised her, she had escaped unwanted attention.

She arrived at Guy's apartment shortly before eleven. The cassette played Lou Reed. She waited for twenty-five minutes then out he came ambling forth. Into the Ford. Downtown. Into the garage.

Twenty minutes later she was pursuing his motorbike heading westside. The stop at Riders. The same wait. And then, the riverside warehouse, the forbidden territory. Guy disappeared, as she hoped, into a black hole amidst the comings and goings of other figures.

She parked. Got out. Breathed deeply. Counted to ten. Then followed.

Inside was unlike anything Anne-Marie had ever seen before, had ever imagined. Inside was vast, thousands upon thousands of square, derelict feet. Rubble and chaos. Beams hanging down. Light entering through open pockets all along the sides. Lit cigarettes torching the space. And everywhere she looked, every corner her eyes glimpsed, there were figures.

Prowling and waiting and hoping and groping and groaning and groining.

Anne-Marie was frozen. It would now be impossible to track down Guy. There were too many people, too many dark corners, too much activity. Still she could not simply stand there like a statue. She decided to walk straight ahead of her into the very middle of the warehouse in an absolute straight line.

No-one bothered her, no-one could possibly suspect, or probably care. Eyes met hers as well as they might in such darkness and when she dared to look back at whoever had passed her, they were always looking back at her. She had her charms even in this remote place. She imagined herself to have the appeal of a youngish man, a slender but firm figure, strong in his own aura. She behaved like a voyeur. This gave her the right to be present while allowing her that certain distance. Huddled in various corners were small groups of people, twos, threes sometimes sixes. She walked on, the air held the stench of drugs, booze, sex, but she could not ascertain what was taking place, until she pushed herself closer to the pulse of the building.

Feeling ashamed Anne-Marie decided she had no business there, she was behaving no better than a peeping Tom. She did not belong. Let them do as they desired, as they pleased, what concern was it of hers? It had been Guy who had captured her imagination and now he was lost to her.

On reaching the door that would lead her back to her Stratos Blue Ford, to transport her to her comfortable, if distraught life, she noticed a stairway leading to another level. More people. People with a different sensibility. Those ascending did so with an urgency. Those descending with a sense of satisfaction. Up she went.

She did not know what had emboldened her but she did know she must go further, or else she would never know why she had done any of this. Upstairs the layout was different. The area was divided into rooms, once offices she supposed, their walls now decaying or destroyed and the roof entirely gone, enabling the moon to shine in brightly. Enabling her to see these men, these night wanderers, bunched and hunched together enjoying one another's bodies, one another's tastes. Anne-Marie felt urgent, but shocked to see such an open display of sex. The sound of orgasm echoed about her ears, its smell pervaded the building. The stench of sweat and need was all about her.

She felt a firm wandering hand about her buttocks and let out a small yelp which disgusted the owner who moved on. She did not know where to go, how to behave. She lacked the guts to turn back, the stamina to go on. All the resources she had grown to discover and set to use were now no good. This was a topsy-turvy world where all her breeding was meaningless, where regular social behaviour was unnecessary. She did not feel threatened in the sense of violence. This was not a world of aggression. It was a world of sex, nothing save sex. Between consenting males. And somewhere in this world was Guy.

The flow of hungry men continued to brush past her and Anne-Marie did not know whether to feel angry, hurt, or humiliated. Confused certainly. She had felt erotic when she first saw Guy in his gear clambering aboard his cycle, horny when she idolised herself in front of the mirrors, but she was now baffled and extremely nervous.

Slowly and carefully she descended the stairs with head downward bent to avoid any confrontation. Men continued to arrive. No-one bothered her. No-one would notice her. She got to the car and with a trembling hand pushed the key into the lock.

Still trembling, a full thirty minutes later, Anne-Marie poured herself a generous vodka on the rocks. She gulped greedily at the drink.

She went into the bathroom to wash herself and catching sight of her leather reflection in the full length mirror, her trembling turned to a tremor of quite a different kind. She once again, or maybe still, felt erotic, sensual, horny. She ran her hand over her breasts down onto the leather of her pants, wet her lips with her tongue, allowed her hand to rest in the area of her crotch. It was time, she decided, to have another vodka.

She woke up Sunday morning from an excellent sleep, the best she had had since his death. She awoke as Anne-Marie, not hiding, not running away, escaping; simply as Anne-Marie whole and real.

That evening her children would arrive home from their grandmother's house and Anne-Marie would begin that gradual process of rebuilding their three lives. Whatever flights of fancy she had encountered this past month were over and done with. She had realised that there was much in the world that did not concern her, that she could never comprehend. It was best to leave this 'much' well alone.

Anne-Marie dressed and went for a walk in Central Park. It was a beautiful day, hot and sunny, with a clear sky. The park was already crowded, joggers, families, dogs, en-routers. She walked south past the zoo breathing deeply, feeling healthy, relaxed. She arrived at a little square opposite the Plaza Hotel. She found a space on a bench. She would sit for quarter of an hour or so before walking home up Fifth Avenue. Tomorrow she would return the car, throw away her foolish costume, discard her fancy role.

Many people buzzed around Anne-Marie in that little square on that Sunday morning in June. But one particular person, yet again, broke her concentration, interrupted her peace, ruined her clarity.

Sitting opposite Anne-Marie, on another bench, was the very same young woman. The one she continually saw. With a sudden burst of anger Anne-Marie rose from her bench and approached the young woman.

"What is it you want?" she asked.

The young woman's head slowly rose, her eyes meeting Anne-Marie's, a piercing look of hatred, unconcealed, hitting out at Anne-Marie.

"Why are you following me? Who are you? What do you want? What are you doing here?"

Still nothing. Nothing for Anne-Marie to grasp.

With further frustration "Why? What is it?"

"Hey, Lady, leave the young miss alone. She ain't doing you no harm," came a voice from behind.

Anne-Marie swung round and came face to face with the tramp in the wig.

"You!" she exclaimed. "Oh leave me alone the pair of you," and with tears rising she started to run home.

She ran all the way to her apartment, a good ten blocks, crying all the time. She did not understand what business these people had with her, what they wanted. Why had her husband died? Was there no-one she could turn to?

Standing in front of her bathroom mirror, her eyes puffy and red, her nose damp and dirty, her head filling with self-pity, Anne-Marie decided that she could not give up the only friend she had. Her male friend. Her male nature. Her secret life must continue for a little longer. Because, for a little longer, she would still be unable to face up to all the pain she was ignoring.

The following Friday night Anne-Marie, with cap suitably peaked, locked the door of her car and walked toward the entrance of the warehouse. The figure to step into the doorway directly ahead of her was Guy Richards. He walked immediately to the stairway and climbed up. She did the same. He arrived upstairs and was beautifully lit by the full moon. She was struck by Guy's image, clad in this erotic fashion.

He walked across the rubble and debris and headed toward a long and precarious catwalk, a rusty metal handrail was the only object for Anne-Marie to clutch at as she nervously followed him. He arrived at the end of the catwalk in a room walled on three sides, no ceiling, and in the middle of one wall a vast and un-paned window overlooking the Hudson. Guy walked directly to the window, looked out across the river, swung around and stood in a provocative fashion. Waiting.

Anne-Marie, who had lingered on the extremity of the room felt that she had now gone too far. Guy was surely expecting her to cross the room and approach his body, kiss his mouth, touch his chest. She stood and watched him as another figure brushed past her, approached Guy, touched him immediately below the waist, and within several moments had fallen to his knees. Before Anne-Marie had time to cry out, to go, to think anything, another figure arrived, and another. They stood and watched the procedure as Anne-Marie stood and watched them. Before too long, one of the newer figures pushed the kneeling man out of position and took his place. More characters arrived to enjoy and participate or merely watch this ritual. And all of the time a look of sheer splendour, highlighted by the full moon, fell over Guy's face. Anne-Marie observing, with open mouth, was quite bewildered. So that was the secret quality Guy Richards harboured.

"What fun these boys have!" she laughed to herself, and taking off her peaked cap with complete abandon she frisbeed it within an inch of Guy Richards' grinning nose and out into the water beyond.

She strode confidently back along the catwalk realising that life was rare and must be lived.

"Dear, sweet, secretive, special Guy," she thought.

And as she thought this she wondered how many secrets her husband may have had, may have died and disappeared with him. He was gone and she was to go on. Though never again would she be quite so bored when Guy Richards broke into talk of stocks and shares.

Still laughing, Anne-Marie pressed firmly on the gas pedal and made her final return journey uptown in that Stratos Blue Ford Mustang.

·····

PART THREE

Alexandra could not get up. The more she tried to persuade herself to stretch her laziness into some active shape, the more she longed to remain asleep, cosseted beneath her covers.

Nothing could disturb her now, she had waited patiently for this sleep, to lie next to this woman. Her English Rosemary. She could rest now, lie peaceful, tonight too, and the next and the next and the next.

It was these thoughts that made her feel so warm, so content, so sleepy. She did not, could not even, stretch across to touch Rosemary. That was how lazy she was, that was how sure, how ignorant.

She had suffered many relationships, many tests, many trials. And then for a long, a very long time she had lived alone, shed all complications, all passion. Life, if a little empty, was easy then. Now she was ready for a new relationship, another marriage of sorts. And here she was lying next to her chosen partner. She made a small grunting sound, a pleasant noise, an expression of content and felt her own two arms embrace herself, a good feeling. She was still asleep. Nothing was troubling her. Sensing Rosemary's warm light breathing close to her, Rosemary's delicate presence, Alexandra could bring herself to do nothing save sleep.

The next thing she knew she was awake. Waking up, feeling

hungry, almost famished. She leant across to gently stroke Rosemary's back. To contact her morning love on this their first morning. She leant a little further. A little further still. Rosemary was not there.

"She must be making breakfast for us both. Eggy little snacks. Baby toasts. Hot liquid." Just what Alexandra had been wanting. Someone to wake up with. Someone to prepare little breakfasts. Lady-like trays.

Still yawning, rubbing sleepy eyes, stretching aching limbs. Alexandra rose from her palatial bed high above Madison and Seventy Eighth Street, took a tiny pee, brushed her baby-shaped whitey-white teeth, pulled on a solid dressing gown and crossed to the kitchen to find her love. "Rosemary," she called, then hollered. "Rosemary," she whispered then pleaded. But silence. No Rosemary, no small eggy breakfast, no companion, no little woman, no-one.

Scanning for notes, searching for clues, desperate for anything, she could manage to find nothing at all. She became frantic, called Rosemary's number, it rang and it rang and it rang.

She started to rifle her apartment for an item of clothing, a billet-doux, a fragment. She opened closets and drawers, trunks and sacks. But nothing. She turned the bed upside down, examined the sheets, the pillow slips, the coverlets. A faint odour. There was nothing else of Rosemary left in the apartment.

Alexandra stood close to her front door hoping to feel close to the outside world and in some way close to Rosemary. She wanted to cry, but she could not. Rosemary had not merely slipped off for an hour, or disappeared for the day even; she was gone, forever gone. Alexandra knew that. But why should she run away like that? Rosemary was a tortured creature. Alexandra knew that, but why had she run? And why was there nothing of Rosemary left behind?

Hugging her front door, Alexandra's perplexed eyes fell upon the table in the hall. She immediately sensed something, smelt something of Rosemary's perfume in the air. There was something missing. She stared hard at the table for several minutes and then knew, knew that Rosemary had taken her gun.

Skipping the eggy breakfast, clutching at clothes, racing through possibilities, Alexandra was quickly on the streets, rushing down Fifth Avenue. Or should she go up? Up down. Down up. Where was the sense? Rosemary would definitely have gone down. Downtown.

She raced ahead, crossing streets, examining people, passers-by, walkers, joggers, shoppers, doers. Suddenly ahead of her she saw a large crowd, a great gathering. Sirens, ambulances, squad cars. Christ! Please no!

Alexandra got to Seventy First Street and could get no further, the block was cordoned off. People stared and chattered on the surrounding street. A shooting? A massacre? Armed robbery? A White House official assassinated? Much conjecture. Some said Jackie O, others Betsy Bloomingdale, some even said the Pope. Yes male, definitely male, caucasian, late thirties. "Thankyou God," said Alexandra, "thankyou for that. Not Rosemary."

But that gun? The sudden disappearance? The shooting? Weren't there always shootings in New York? Weren't the streets paved and littered with crime?

She felt this was a waste of time. This had nothing to do with Rosemary. Nothing at all. She leant forward.

"Anyone arrested?"

"No. They ain't got no-one. An invisible crime. Fella shot dead and no gunman. That's this city for ya."

Alexandra felt relieved, she moved on. *No gunman.* Those were the words. Rosemary had been acquitted, wasn't Alexandra simply over-reacting? Panicking? Go to Rosemary's apartment. Go there now. That is where she is. Of course. Alexandra went to Rosemary's apartment. There was no-one home.

Alexandra had been just seventeen when she first married. A devastatingly handsome Argentinian, a breeder of horses, a wealthy man from a wealthy family. And sex mad. Sex all the time. Morning noon and night. Hung like one of his stallions. He had not been a good lover. Not Max. She meant little to him. Eighteen months later they were divorced. A scandal in Buenos Aires.

She ran away, left that life behind, abandoned Buenos Aires. She went to California, took a job, rented an apartment, stayed two years. Travelled to Europe, lived in Paris for a year or more, ran an art gallery, well, and successfully.

It was there that she had first met her second husband. An English artist, a good bit older than her, an eccentric sort. Long hair almost white. Smoked a small pipe filled with hashish, recited poetry, played opera very loudly as he painted his large canvases, *Gauginesque*. Native girls in vivid colours.

They lived in Maida Vale, a place in London. He had tired of his travels. He wished to settle for English greys. They went to large dinner parties, drank champagne, rose at midday. They were a team.

Then on the eve of her twenty-fifth birthday an older woman, Irish, with great beauty but flawed eyes had seduced her with romantic talk.

They met, constantly. The woman wrote novels, well, and successfully. They took tea together, walked the city over and over, lived in galleries, attended matinees. Their friendship delved deep. it challenged them both. This platonic relationship.

Her marriage lasted for several more years. The Irish writer went to live in Mexico. Alexandra began to have affairs with women, physical relationships. At the age of thirty she again divorced and came to live in New York City. She again ran an art gallery, Upper East Side. She earned good money, bought stocks and shares. They boomed.

Her second husband Alfred died, and to her amazement he left her lots of money. Alexandra had done well. She was a materially secure woman, and for the past year or more had ceased working entirely. her stocks and shares secured her lifestyle. She wanted to write, she tried to write, but she wasn't awfully good. She didn't have 'it'.

She realised there was no use standing outside Rosemary's

apartment for the rest of her life. She had waited there an hour already, remembering. She moved on. Moving away from Rosemary and her apartment, Alexandra acknowledged how angry she felt at the world. Why had she done this to her? Why had this happened to her? She jumped into a cab and rode uptown on Eighth.

"Leave me at Times Square."

Burrows, Joseph, grunted, left her at Times Square.

She found one of those dark bars that have a tendency to harbour those dark types.

"Bourbon on the rocks."

"All yours." The barman served. The bum approached.

"Hey, beautiful, interested in checking out a good time?"

"Go clean the streets."

Alexandra was not going to hide her anger from the world. Let it out, let them all see it. She made a huge, unattractive sound, a groaning bound to raise attention. The barman grinned, the bum retreated.

"There's a girl who knows what's what."

She turned sharply to find the voice and came eye to eye with a bedraggled looking fellow in a ridiculous black wig.

"Ha!" she scorned, "Another bourbon . . . and one for my friend. Howdy. Care for a stool? And a drink? Care for either?"

"Yeah both. Yeah both."

He sat alongside her, a curious figure, smelling of the streets and endless wandering. She felt this fellow had been searching for a good while now. She felt this man had visited many places, many ports, all to no avail. They were silent as they sipped their iced bourbons. She had sat in other rooms with this man. She had seen his wig upon the floor, his dirty pot-marked crown. He had occurred in many dreams, a figure of *déjà-vu*.

Looking about her, seeing his paper bags about him on the floor, an old trolley – sort of push-chair – she recognised this Mother Courage. She knew that he, like her, had dug deep into the pit of his stomach, the recess of his bowels and come up with nothing, nothing save pain, old pain. They were connected by their lack of power, their inability to change themselves.

As a small girl she had been given all she desired, she had been spoilt. This rearing served her poorly in later life, she was not able to combat the perpetual struggle. This fellow had chosen not to. They did not speak, they had no need. They moved on.

Hitting the streets the blare of traffic and harsh daylight smote them. He led her eastwards past the tramps and hustlers, the lady-like black whores, the tireless pimps, the checkered tourists queueing for yet another 'show'. She was tired of walking alone. For days and weeks, possibly months before she had met Rosemary she had walked alone. To the movies, an occasional bar, the park, looking for, waiting for. Her life had become an everlasting bore. Not working gave little meaning to her days. She had so few friends in New York, so few interested her. Her new companion became quite chatty on the streets, full of personality. He did not speak to her, it was to the passing world he addressed his elusive, incoherent remarks. Alexandra was content to tag along, just happy to be there.

Once, a few months earlier, when she was at her most bored, she had gone to one of those live sex shows in a squalid room in a filthy block right off Times Square. It resembled the one they were presently passing. Times Square was rife with simulation. People selling goods purporting to be what, in reality, they were not. New York was beginning to disgust Alexandra. To have found and lost Rosemary in so short a space of time, seemed to defy all reason, an act of supreme and arrant carelessness. It was too stupid.

True, she was a forgetful person, prone to lose belongings, a trifle absent-minded. She had once lost a neighbour's dog for an entire afternoon when she had been entrusted to dog-sit. Never again.

She had once lost her husband for three solid hours in a department store when they were on a shopping spree. And then she had found him. But to have lost a lover, a newly found and much needed lover, surely crossed all borders of misfortune and bore no resemblance, begged no comparison with any previous misdemeanours.

It could be possible, perhaps, that Rosemary had a long-standing commitment, a prior arrangement though she surely would have left word to indicate this, left something. Surely?

No! Something urgent had happened to Rosemary. Some drama had stepped in her way. "Let's go in here," she said to the Wigman.

They stepped inside the purple and burgundy foyer to be greeted by the smell of stale, of rot.

"Two please."

She pushed her dollars inside the glass booth and received two crinkle-ended stubs.

"A cheap production," thought Alexandra.

Inside was certainly cheap, cheap and not cheerful, cheap and faded. The Wigman had pulled his perambulator up the stairway to the intimate theatre. Broken velvet chairs in need of re-springing were haphazardly arranged in a dozen or so rows. Two other clients were seated gaping at the sordid fleshy act badly in need of a spring clean.

The Wigman, mentally stimulated by this scenario, began to chatter furiously. Angry stares and snorts came his way from the couple in the stalls and the onstage twosome. Alexandra found it all most diverting, and that was the very thing she needed. A complete diversion. Anything that might distract her from the Rosemary mystery would be welcome.

She looked up from her wanderings to witness a vile charade of simulated copulation.

Loud and burping disco-music thumped through the beat-up speakers. The players shimmied their sateen'd asses across the black planks groaning un-convincingly even for a matinée.

"Come on Wiggy," she called out. He was addressing a faded poster of a fading sex starlet on the brown and tattered hessian wall.

"El splito."

They left.

Outside it was early afternoon and Alexandra suddenly yearned to cry. She wanted to sob and sob but knew she could not, not there and then.

"I'll see you around amigo," she mumbled. "I'm going home to weep."

The Wigman broke into a terrific guffaw and looking pleased as punch he shook Alexandra's hand with great ferocity and ambled chuckling eastward.

"Don't look at what you were," Alexandra thought the following day when she awakened. She rubbed her arms but they felt like a strangers. She twisted her neck and rotated her head but it seemed to float off, away.

She telephoned Rosemary, there was no reply. Rosemary had gone. It was as if she had never existed or been a part of Alexandra's life. She contemplated the ugly possibility, that Rosemary had killed herself. She had, after all, stolen that gun and rushed off without explanation. Was Rosemary the type to do such a thing? To commit suicide. Alexandra thought long and hard. Tried to remember Rosemary as vividly as possible, found she could barely remember Rosemary at all. She could see her face, her figure, her physical appearance, but she was unable to remember her spirit, her interior being, her character.

Alexandra got up and stepped inside the shower. Her body smelt vaguely unpleasant, as bodies do after a great deal of crying, of releasing the pain, the poison.

She dried herself and drank some orange juice. She did not know what to do, how to begin her day. She wanted to go to Rosemary's apartment but she worried that she was being stupid, deceiving herself. Rosemary had wanted to move on and had done so, no mystery, no drama.

She went to Rosemary's apartment and hung around. She waited all day. She saw people come and go, neighbours, visitors of neighbours, deliverers, dogs and cats, the occasional bat.

She went home and cried herself to sleep again.

The next day she got up and went to Rosemary's apartment. She hung around all day. She went home.

The following day the same. And the day after that. And still no Rosemary. No sign, no clue, no smell. She had gone without trace.

Rosemary had vanished. That night Alexandra could not sleep at all. She was haunted by a restlessness. The restlessness that is brought about by indecision.

The following morning she had made up her mind. She would have to move forward. She was forced to accept this situation for what it was. She could not enter any further into it, the search, the longing, the remembrance, they would have to be left behind. Like Buenos Aires they must become a part of her past.

She ate a rigorous breakfast, scrubbed her back in the bathtub and strode across the park. Alexandra found herself wandering on the Upper West Side. Crossing a particular block she watched a line of rather luxurious limousines pulling up outside a grand and Gothic building. It was a crematorium, and stepping out of the first limousine she saw an elegant and self-contained young woman, followed by her young children.

"Poor dear," thought Alexandra, "another woman in weeds." She derived a certain comfort from this, a camaraderie. She felt less alone. Arriving at the end of the block she was greeted with:

"Big funeral. 'Portant folks."

"You!" She laughed. And there stood the Wigman, dolls and all, mac filthier than ever. She shook his hand. They walked on, northbound, side by side in silence. "Let's go in here amigo."

They had arrived at a precinct and Alexandra confidently led the unsure Wigman into the heart of the police-station. Noise, stench of disinfectant, ringing telephones, activity was the general greeting. The Wigman did not care for these surroundings, rather like a small child he tried to break away, to sneak off on his own.

"You wait there," commanded Alexandra. She wanted to enquire about a missing person. She had to queue. Directly ahead of her, in the queue, attached by hand-cuffs to a burly officer was a frightening looking criminal, half-woman, half-man, in heavy make-up carrying a kit bag with the word KARATE printed boldly across. Apparently, this creature had stabbed an old lady on a Hundreth Street with a gardening fork. The wound had not been deep, the prongs being too thick and blunt to penetrate, but nevertheless a bloody and macabre act. The Karate person made no comment, took no interest in the exchange of information passing between Burly and the desk officer. Eventually the Karate person was led toward a series of sinister corridors, a place where Alexandra hoped never to venture.

Alexandra gave details of Rosemary's appearance, physical, and disappearance, actual, – omitting the weapon – to the desk sergeant and together they filled in the appropriate form to be circulated amongst the other Manhattan precincts. That, it would seem, was that.

Throughout this the Wigman stood by staring in alarm at the uniformed gathering of ladies and gentlemen buzzing and ambling about. All the while he registered the fear of a lost child.

"Come on," she beckoned, and they left.

They continued northward through Harlem, silence dividing and binding them.

"It is useless," she thought, "to walk with this man to the edge of this island. Life is a series of disappointments and anything else that occurs in-between is temporary and to be relished for the fleeting time it will take before becoming its own shadow and then disappearing without trace, without leaving a clear memory of itself, an imprint. All that remains of a person who had been and gone in one's life was a mental impression, generally unreliable, romanticised or fuzzy."

They passed through street after Harlem street, occasionally pointed at, mostly ignored. The day was now hot and Alexandra imagined the island to be a stage she could jump from and the auditorium below a swimming pool to plop into.

It was neither. It was nothing save land and ocean and if she had wings to jump she would surely damage them in the downward flight and consequently drown in the crash landing that would follow. She would then be sentenced to the bottom of the ocean to wander for eternity, banished to the fish kingdom without hope of finding her English Rosemary.

Alexandra began to sweat and put her hand to her gills, that is neck, to wipe away the warm moist trickle.

Her feet and fins were becoming terribly sore and the constant babble the Wigman had fallen into began to make her eardrums pound. The scales on her face felt as if they might flake away and her mouth would simply not refrain from opening and closing.

"Come on little lady, say you' prez."

Alexandra started from the nightmare where her wandering mind had misled her and saw she was now at the northern tip of Manhattan, at the medieval place called the Cloisters. She knelt down and offered up a small prayer. She asked for peace of mind and begged for Rosemary to be firmly placed in her past. For the haunting to cease.

In her mind she lit a million candles, each one demanding the restoration of her cherished sanity.

"Got to get the bus," old Wiggy wheezed. The morning's marathon having wounded his chest.

"Wanna come?"

"Where are you going?" she asked, more her old Argentinian self.

"Got to go downtown. Down Battery. Got a rendez, 'nother little lady I know. Meets me there. Other end o' town. Got to get the bus. Wanna come?"

"Taxi!" the Argentinian hollered. "No. Thanks all the same. I'm leaving this place. Selling up. I'm off to Europe. Morocco maybe. Got to pack."

The Wigman howled with a desperate bronchial wheeze. This woman was the funniest he had ever known, he shook his head and wiped away the sort of tear a fierce wind induces.

"Great woman. Great woman."

"Not a bad old fish yourself."

Alexandra climbed into the yellow cab as the Wigman headed toward the bus-stop, repeating, "great woman," before spiralling off into a new monologue.

"Where to, lady?"

Alexandra looked into her purse and produced a small pocket diary. She searched for the name of the whizz-kid financier who had been so highly recommended. Ah! Richards, Guy Richards. There he was. That was it. Fifty Eighth Street at Madison.

"Fifty Eighth and Madison if you please. I'm going to sell me some shares. Make me a killing. I'm leaving this town."

Burrows, Joseph, merely grunted, merely drove her to Fifty Eighth Street and Madison Avenue.

.....

PART FOUR

Guy Richards parked his motorbike in its lot at the pay-garage and prepared to change from his heavy leather gear into his Lacoste leisurewear.

"Fuck it!" he thought, and climbed into his Stratos Blue Ford dressed as he was.

He felt he had had enough of all this. All this hero-worship, all this pretence. Besides, the world was full of cranks. Only tonight some loony had thrown a cap at him whilst he was being serviced. Jealous little wreck. It had almost bruised his nose, his beautiful nose. The world was full of weirds.

Besides, he missed James. It was less than a month since he had been so brutally shot down on the streets of the city, a huge loss. Guy and James had been lovers for almost a year. James, in effect, was a happily married man, but like so many men something in his marriage confined him. James had been having an affair with a young woman for six years. The affair had become painful and James had chosen to end it. For six years he had had the strength to keep the affair clandestine but at the time of parting he had weakened and turned to Guy for comfort. He told Guy that his mistress was beautiful but he felt she was losing touch with reality, becoming remote. He could not leave Anne-

Marie, his wife, at least he chose not to.

For many nights after many hard days work the two men had stayed up late talking, getting drunk. Then one particular night they had become a little too inebriated and Guy had suggested James should stay over at his apartment. James had readily agreed, telephoned Anne-Marie, who was already snoozing in her Henri Bendel negligée, and the two men had fallen giggling onto Guy's queen size bedspread upon his queen size bed.

That had been the start of something new. Quite extraordinary as the two men had known each other for a number of years and neither had recognised this tendency in the other. Although it must be said for every minute they had known each other Guy had always been a little in love with James.

James, with his super fine jaw-line, his ivory white teeth, those Paul Newman eyes, that golden wavy hair, his athletic yet yielding body, his easy personality, his genius for amassing fortunes, wasn't he just the All-American dreamboy? Everybody's elder brother, every teenager's major crush?

He was certainly Guy's 'Numero Uno'. Guy, himself no ugly duckling, who could have had every man, woman, or dog on Manhattan crawling across the island to bed him.

Guy Richards had been orphaned at the age of fourteen. He had been fostered by George and Betty Charlesworth, a young elderly couple full of joy and vitality, not wealthy but not without generosity. They doted on the boy, sacrificed all in order to give to him, and lavished more tender loving care than any balanced human has any right to wish for.

When Guy was in his early twenties, having achieved brilliant success at college, George and Betty, exactly seventy each, had died within three months of one another, a respective stroke and a respectable heart attack.

This had left Guy alone in the world, a solitary person with no-one to cater for and nobody to answer to. As a child he had always been a loner, never easily making friends, so this position suited him exactly. Guy was not prone to morbid moods, to self pity or self destruction. That is not to say he did not have a dark side to his nature. But this *other*, this darkness, was something he controlled. When Guy Richards spent the evening alone he would crack open a quarter bottle of Veuve-Cliquot, always the quarter, and listen to Schubert for solo piano on his compact disc player. In more frisky spirit he would down a Becks Beer and play Bob Dylan or Charlie Sexton, check himself out in the mirror, cruise his own image, push gel through his hair, rub baby oil on those parts he cared to caress for hours on end.

6.30 a.m. and Guy was pulling up outside of his apartment in Murray Hill. Hoping that no-one he knew would see him dressed this way, he swiftly entered his building and sprinted up the stairs to his apartment on the second floor.

Once inside his steel and grey home, Guy made directly for the mega-refrigerator in his Italian kitchen and slugged from a carton of chocolate milk. Being careful enough to switch off all the bells on all the telephones he then pulled off his huge, heavyweight, leather boots, unzipped himself from his shining armour of leather trousers, leather jacket, brushed cotton vest, threw aside his wide band elasticated jock strap, swallowed half a valium, and climbed under his charcoal-grey corduroy bedspread in amongst his Perry Ellis bed linen to fall, albeit anxiously, to sleep.

Guy was hounded by a variety of dreams that morning. He dreamt of James, of Anne-Marie, of things he could not recall, but above all he dreamt of those threatening letters which he continued to receive. And more alarming still he dreamt that James was the author of these notes. He awoke at 11.50 a.m. in a cold and clammy sweat. He determined that things would have to change. He must stop going on these night prowls, these all-night benders.

He poured some freshly squeezed orange juice, made a pot of coffee and checked his telephone service. Only one call, from Anne-Marie.

"Damn," thought Guy, "what does she want on a Sunday?" This was the second time in recent weeks that she had telephoned. It was not that he disliked Anne-Marie, he was immensely fond of her, it was just that he couldn't handle her since James had died. In truth he had been unable to really face her since the two men had begun their affair. Previously he had been almost close to Anne-Marie, they were almost attracted to one another, though nothing beyond the mildest flirtation had ever occurred. Then, during the term of the illicit affair, Guy had avoided her as much as possible. He and James had spent more time together than he could ever have dreamt. Quite often James had skipped going to his country home at weekends in order to remain with Guy at his apartment. The two men played squash together, showered together, getting as worked up as possible together, as much as one could in the showers of the Racquet Club, returned to Murray Hill together, and slowly but surely stripteased around the place, sportsmen discarding their unwanted garb, until they were both naked and crawling across each others flesh.

They would take business dinners in their finely tailored suits in grand Manhattan restaurants and behave with fierce decorum until that moment when too much St. Emilion had been drunk and one of them would start to make discreet yet horny little signs across the table linen, creating impatience in the air, which always led to the bed linen on Murray Hill. Then home to the wife. Little wonder that Anne-Marie made Guy feel uneasy.

The first letter that Guy received, had arrived exactly twenty four hours after James had been gunned down. "I KNEW ALL ABOUT YOU AND HIM." Guy automatically assumed that the murderer had sent it and felt he should go directly to the police. But he did not, he could not come into the open and jeopardise his brilliant career which relied so heavily upon the super-wealthy 'straight' community of Manhattan. He could not watch Anne-Marie suffer the humiliation and pain of discovering this truth. And then came the second letter: "HOW CAN YOU BE SURE THAT SHE DOESN'T, OR WON'T KNOW?"

Guy had never found it easy coming to terms with the fact that he was gay, and because he was a loner and did not feel he was seeking a companion of either sex he had decided to postpone the acknowledgement that he was sexually 'anything'. He simply 'did' as he wished. The relationship with James had been unique. Unique for Guy as he had never had a relationship with anyone before. He had never even really had a best friend. Unique for James as he had never had any physical contact with any man before. The turmoil and need that brought them together was a happy coincidence.

Upon receipt of the second letter Guy had sold various stocks and unit trusts and opened a deposit account in a downtown branch of the Chemical Bank to prepare for the inevitable demands for money. He waited and waited and daily his account accrued interest but no such request was forthcoming. Then one day a note arrived. "LUSCIOUS IN LEATHER THAT'S WHAT YOU ARE."

"Jesus," thought Guy, "a major fucking crank." Guy started to feel followed, observed, and started to fear for his own life. But the midnight feasts were his way of coping with the loneliness and grief he felt at James' death. His peculiar way of mourning his lover. Besides, the late night warehouse where he feasted was not as ferocious as an outsider might imagine and to be passive in fellatio qualified, for him at least, as safe sex.

Guy ran a deep hot bath and decided not to call Anne-Marie until he felt more able to deal with her. Soaking in the luxuriant sudded water Guy now realised he was feeling paranoid. Paranoid about his gay activities. Paranoid about the letters, though he had received none for an entire week. Paranoid about Anne-Marie, about her very existence. Paranoid that she should find out he was gay. Paranoid that anyone should find out he was gay. Paranoid that he should find out he was gay.

He soaked for a whole hour and more until he decided that he would not go back to the warehouse.

Feeling good, a clean almost new man, he telephoned Anne-Marie. She was mumbling something about meeting and Guy urgently wanted to tell her that like a good boy he would never go back to the warehouse, as if this would absolve all, wipe clean the slate and enable him to start again. But as Anne-Marie knew nothing of such activities, even in her wildest imaginings, he feebly wittered on about stocks and shares, her children and blah, blah, blah. Their loss of the same man separated them and built a lack of communication. Then Guy realised that Anne-Marie was actually suggesting they meet. This was a breakthrough for she had closeted herself up since James' death, and now she was trying to make a dinner appointment.

Guy placed a Schubert for solo piano compact disc upon his player, brewed a cup of English tea and decided to potter about his apartment for the rest of the day.

Tomorrow he was to lunch with his new client, an Argentinian woman named Alexandra. Guy liked her. Already they had formed a friendship. Lunch was something he could look forward to.

Alexandra first stepped into Guy's office the afternoon of James' cremation. It was a difficult day for Guy, a day when he would have preferred to have stayed at Murray Hill crying. But as Anne-Marie had cancelled brunch, not feeling up to it herself, Guy had decided to take the bull by the horns and return to work.

Alexandra had no appointment. Guy had been in the men's room for practically an hour. Having a little weep. He had barely returned to his office when in swept the bold Alexandra, hotly pursued by a secretary in modest consternation.

"I need to sell!" she exclaimed. "Masses!"

It turned out that she had known James, had met him once at a high powered Manhattan party and he had recommended Guy in glowing terms. Guy told Alexandra the news regarding James and she had been suitably shocked. He then told her the circumstances and she looked slightly shattered. He went on to relate the when and whereabouts and Alexandra looked nothing short of appalled and burst out crying. Guy had hoped she was laughing as any form of excessive behaviour embarrassed him, and although laughter would have been socially wrong, crying was a positive faux-pas. He was, in spite of himself, touched by this display.

He and Alexandra dined together that night and she confided in him to such a degree that he felt almost related to her. She overwhelmed him, with the disclosure that she was gay. Guy felt quite ashamed at his own inadequacy, his abiding weakness to resist any similar admission.

Poor Alexandra was nursing a broken heart, a love affair with a beautiful if remote younger woman, who had simply disappeared from the face of the earth. An uncanny occurrence that had left Alexandra so beside herself that she had determined to sell up and move on.

After this first evening, Guy and Alexandra met weekly, always dining together in this or that Manhattan restaurant, Guy picking up the tab, Alexandra regaling him with tales of her life, her time in Paris, London, Buenos Aires. With her tight and angry curls, her almost mosaic nose, her aluminium complexion, she seemed invincible, a war goddess, heroine, Boadicea of her time, but to Guy with each consecutive supper she became frail, a more fragile being altogether than even Anne-Marie, struck by the grief of a husband's death.

Alexandra and Guy were somehow bound together in their mutual loss of love, and this binding suited them both. In the weeks that followed their initial meeting, Guy made money for Alexandra. She was already familiar with the accumulation of wealth. Her first husband Max had settled handsome sums at the time of their divorce, and Alfred, her next marriage, had left behind marvellous amounts. She was a woman who knew how to accumulate. But this miracle that Guy performed was quite something else. Every day he sold another stock, a new share, more of her trusts and each day her bank account fattened. Alexandra might have become a rather gluttonous woman amidst such excitement, such sums.

Guy, oblivious to the financial wizardry he was displaying, continued his life. Work every weekday, incorporating five business lunches Monday to Friday. Squash twice a week, Tuesday and Thursday. The odd business dinner, the odd female date, the odd movie, his treasured dinner with Alexandra and then every weekend to his warehouse haunt for that forbidden jaunt.

"Is this life after death for Guy Richards?" he asked himself. "Is there life after death?" he wondered. Was James presently in the heavenly meadows, that perfect place we all dream of though none are able to describe? Was it a Christian existence that James was passing through? Emulating Christ? Turning other cheeks? Helping fellow angels? Or was he wandering limbo-like through unexplained meadow after unanswered field?

He went to bed that night, a much troubled man. Swallowing a whole valium, twice his usual and occasional dosage, he fell quite furiously to sleep.

The following morning, after a whole night dreaming he had turned into a killer whale, Guy awoke to open a letter saying: "GOODBYE BUENOS AIRES, BIENVENUE TANGIER."

Although he had received no letters for a week, he always knew that his crank would be back for more.

He became convinced that this was the work of James' murderer. The letters were so odd, without reason, demand, almost without blackmail.

He threw the letter into his garbage can. Garbage. That was what it was, he would pay no more attention to it, but he could not help being troubled by its existence. Even when the garbage had been removed from the apartment, after it had made its long journey to its destination of final disposal, it would still manage to exist. Even when it was reduced, with all the other garbage to fumes and ashes it would still pollute the air and visit trouble on Guy.

Guy was beginning to suspect that the sender of the letters, the presumed murderer, the prospective blackmailer was perhaps the same woman with whom James had been having an affair . . . a *crime passionel*. She had chosen to disturb the peace around Guy, to disturb the people around James, she was probably blackmailing Anne-Marie, probably haunting her. Should he ask Anne-Marie? It would not be easy as it would raise the topic of Guy's threatening letters and their contents. The only solution was to get to this person, this potential murderess and confront her. He could do two things to achieve this. Firstly he could be passive and wait. Wait for the aggressor to contact him with a request for money, for a meeting, a request for contact. Or, and this seemed preferable, he must contact her. That was what he would do. How? He did not even have a name for this woman.

He did not know of any other person who might know of her existence. He knew that James had told no-one else. Unless Anne-Marie had known all along of this affair and could lead Guy to this woman. If she knew that her husband had had a mistress the chances were likely that she would know about James and Guy. Guy persuaded himself that Anne-Marie could have no such knowledge as her marriage seemed, to the outside world at any rate, without flaw.

He could not go to Anne-Marie with this, he could go to no-one. Although, he longed to tell Alexandra that he was looking for a younger woman whom he believed had shot down James and was now tormenting him.

An interesting and possible solution presented itself, to place an advertisement in The Times, in the personal columns.

On his way that early afternoon to meet Alexandra for their lunch at the Four Seasons, Guy Richards felt pretty pleased with himself.

The advertisement would run the following day:

"GUY DESPERATELY SEEKING CHICK, ME LUSCIOUS YOU ANONYMOUS. WE BOTH KNEW HIM AND SHE DOESN'T KNOW. TANGIER IS HOT AND JAMES WOULDN'T LIKE IT THERE. PLEASE! CALL ME. I MUST MEET WITH YOU!"

Alexandra was already seated when Guy arrived. She had ordered a bottle of Moet & Chandon, her treat, today lunch was on her. The cork popped as Guy sat down.

"Get my note?" she inquired.

"No," said Guy, "what note?"

"I've taken a house in Tangier. It's all turquoise and it has a beautiful pool, a view of the ocean. I leave next month."

Guy started to blush. He had jumped to too many conclusions. It had been Alexandra who had sent that note.

"Oh that note. Yes of course. Congratulations." A pause. "Have you sent me any other un-signed notes?"

"No, of course not. Guy are you alright?"

"Yes fine."

Guy looked rather pale, a touch feeble. He did not seem to be breaking through life at all successfully. She went on to tell him she had a prospective buyer for her Manhattan apartment, a woman with two young children who had been recently widowed and was looking for somewhere a little less grand than her present abode. She had fallen in love with Alexandra's place and a sale appeared promising.

She was throwing out so much of her stuff, her possessions, she would travel light toward Europe, she had stopped craving to know where her friend had got to, she had ceased longing for her, she was a woman on new horizons. They clinked their glasses of champagne to celebrate this news. Alexandra was someone with great energy surging through her, someone released from past bonds, someone who was moving on. The decision to stop searching for her true love, whoever that might be, had given her a re-birth, a creation.

Guy, on the other hand, was beginning to resemble someone whose life was ebbing away. He was turning greyer with each sip of champagne, with each mouthful of wild mushroom salad.

Eventually Guy fainted. He slumped from his chair and fell to the floor. A terrific furore took place inside the restaurant. All conversation stopped for an astonishing period of twenty-two seconds and it seemed as if Manhattan had fallen under the enemy. Following this aghast silence came the most fierce of babblings and slowly the entire restaurant rose to its feet, all talking at once, pointing and reverberating the name of Guy Richards.

Alexandra was at Guy's side, his head held up in her arms requesting some water from a nearby and frightened looking waiter. Slowly Guy began to come round, to revive, and once again a tumultuous silence befell the standing restaurant. Guy looked around him and saw a sea of staring faces and felt quite bewildered. Alexandra helped him to his feet and as he rose to his full height a socially awkward moment telegraphed its way around the restaurant. There was a moment, a mere split second, when the unanimous folk appeared as if they would break into applause, into angry manic clapping. Instead there was a vast clearing of throats, a hugely unnatural starting up of conversation, a great scraping of chairs, and a mass re-seating of the horrified crowd. It was quite simply as if a plague had entered their midst.

Alexandra helped Guy onto the street and the Maitre D' looked glad to see the back of them. The echo of discussion followed them all the way into the taxi and only stopped with the abrupt slamming of the cab door.

Guy looked miserable. Alexandra accompanied him to his apartment and saw him all the way to his bathroom door where Guy politely thanked her and assuring her he would be fine, waved her off.

For the next three hours Guy sat on his lavatory, he was overcome with an inability to move. He felt as if he would never walk again. Everything in life had seized up, everything was tightening around him, allowing him no freedom to breathe, leaving no space in which to expand. He supposed this was all part of the grieving process. But he could not be sure if he were grieving for James' death or for his own miserable life.

After three hours he decided to go to the kitchen where he spent the next two hours sitting on a kitchen stool. His mind was a blank. He could only think about Ms. Anonymous. He urgently felt that she would be able to save his life. If he could only contact James' mistress/murderess he felt he might understand everything and would then be free to extricate himself from this turmoil and start to live again.

After two hours he rose and went to lie on his bed. Climbing on top of his elegant bedspread, still clad in his Versace suit and shirt, Guy Richards fell immediately asleep.

Guy awoke the following morning, after almost twelve hours sleep, at seven o'clock, got up and walked directly into the shower. As the steaming hot water showered forcibly down onto his beautiful if crumpled Versace suit Guy realised he was not yet in that conscious state it is preferable to attain before attacking a working day. He stepped from the shower and threw off his garments, climbed into an aqua towelling bath robe.

He remembered his advertisement and with great excitement rushed out onto the street and travelled the block to the nearby news-stand. He purchased the newspaper.

"Cute way to go about," chuckled Uncle Ed the honest vendor.

Guy did not even hear him, was far beyond realising he was wearing a bath robe in the streets of the city, and would have noticed nothing at all but for the two men on the corner pointing at him.

Back in the safety of his super masculine apartment, Guy scanned the personal columns to find, with great glee, his advertisement, intact, without error, not even a spelling mistake. Guy was pleased, felt good at last. It was now a matter of waiting. He felt sure she would contact him at home. This saviour, this black angel.

At nine o'clock he telephoned his secretary and said he would not be in that day. He could discern an anxious tone at the other end of the line. He believed he could hear his secretary whispering to other colleagues as if he were a wanted criminal and it was her duty to keep him talking so they might trace the call. He hung up and did not contemplate further. These people did not concern him today. He went and sat on the kitchen stool. Two hours and ten minutes later the telephone rang. It was Anne-Marie. She was confirming their dinner plans for the following evening.

She was the last person he wanted to see. "Great, Anne-Marie, terrific, eight thirty then." Followed by a moment of inspiration. "Oh, by the way, there's someone I very much want you to meet. Someone I know you'll get along with."

Exhausted by all this activity, and a little more than depressed by the lack of response from his saviour, Guy went and lay on his bed. He fell asleep. Three hours later the telephone rang. This time it must be her. He knew it. He knew by the way it was ringing that this time it was her. He allowed it to ring for a while longer. It continued to ring. It had to be her. He picked it up. It was Alexandra. She had telephoned the office to discover he was still unwell and she was concerned. Reassuring her that he needed some rest having overdone it at work, he invited her to join him and a friend for dinner the following evening. Taking this as an indication that all was well, for Guy's office staff had given Alexandra quite a different impression, she graciously accepted his offer and arranged to meet at eight thirty that Wednesday night.

She hung up and Guy was relieved to discover he was alone again. All this inactivity was making him listless so he went to lie down on his enormous off-white sofa.

He fell into a deep snooze, then awoke from a dream where he imagined he was drowning at the bottom of a huge Moroccan swimming pool with many Moroccan guards clutching at swords.

As he awoke he tumbled onto the floor and felt a large and healthy erection between his legs. Either the spectacle of many Moroccan guards or the realisation he had not drowned was pumping good solid life through him. He went to the bathroom, threw off his bath robe and drowned his entire body in a full bottle of baby oil.

Three hours later he emerged from his bathroom naked and went and sat on the kitchen stool. He had not eaten for over twenty-four hours, his life was becoming an obsession with doing nothing. His armpits were smelling of an unpleasant odour and his face was badly in need of a shave, his unbrushed teeth were starting to fur and his breath to smell of poison from not having eaten for days.

He opened the fridge and took out a bottle of beer. He drank it. He fell asleep standing against the open refrigerator door, the dim light, half-hidden by the orange juice carton, falling across his strong and well defined male shape. The few hairs on his chest and arms standing to attention amongst an ocean of goose pimples. His penis curving slightly under, napping whilst he took no notice. His two strong, golden brown legs supporting his handsome frame which only served to house his broken heart.

It was midnight when Guy started awake, shivering at the frostiness emanating from the refrigerator and startled by the loud clicking noice of the machine commencing its own de-frosting process. He slammed the door of the fridge and went to lie on the hearth rug of his living room floor. Lighting the coal effect fire and taking a blanket from the closet in the hallway Guy lay down and fell asleep again.

Guy could not understand why he felt so tired but he did not care. It would either pass or it would not, he would continue to vegetate or awaken and revert to the same patterns as before. Or, potentially, he could change.

He was one moment a beetle, the next a sexual warrior, a third drowning, a fourth a suicide, a fifth plant life, a sixth dead. Asleep or awake there was little difference at present.

The next time Guy stirred it was 4 a.m. and the saviour had still not visited him. He got up took a valium and went to bed. He slept well for the next six hours, anxieties abandoning him, imagination escaping.

He awoke realising that he could not attend his office that day. He might never return to his office again.

Guy looked rough, he was finding it difficult to really awaken from such incredible amounts of sleep. He did, however, have a healthy appetite, raiding his refrigerator he toasted English muffins, sizzled Canadian rashers, scrambled American eggs, prepared packet-mix hash brown potatoes, drank gallons of orange juice and brewed a ton of piping hot coffee.

Ordinary human life was starting to pump through him. He devoured his feast and took a shower. He remained in the shower for practically an hour, scrubbing and rubbing himself all over, the hot solid water lashing every part of his being. He washed his hair, worked up a generous lather.

Wrapping himself in bath towels, Guy decided to pour himself a large vodka. A drink he had never indulged in and a habit, to drink at this hour, he had never formed. But this Guy was somehow different from the other Guy Richards. He had conformed too well for too long and was finally acknowledging the troubled adolescence he had ignored. He fleetingly wished he had run his advert in the New York Times for a further day but he had now tired of waiting for this saviour to descend. He would have to look elsewhere.

He played his small collection of rock music at full pitch, threw back the vodka and threw off the towels, threw open all the windows of his apartment, his naked self greeting the hot and humid New York air. It was late June and the temperature was in the nineties, the days sweltering and the nights clammy and the tempers fraying. Guy breathed in the hot air and relished it as if it were the first day of a long vacation, the air sweeter, fresher than any he had known.

He lay on the floor on his large oval mauve rug and laughed. He laughed for a full sixty minutes. It now seemed that every experience Guy underwent took an inordinate amount of time. As if to make up for all the wasted time he had spent rushing hither and thither. Previously his life had worked to mechanical finesse. Everything operating to clockwork. Constantly on time. Now the element of time was changing for Guy. He would take as long as he dared, to do whatever he pleased.

Even his escapades to the warehouse had been set to a pattern. A rigid schedule. These perameters were stifling Guy, driving him crazy. He would have no more to do with them.

He went to his wardrobe and got out his leather gear. He put on his leather jacket over his naked body. He examined himself in front of the mirror. His hair had dried in its own natural curls and flattered him. His stubble was by now quite substantial and made him resemble a model from Italian Vogue, his body was a beautiful thing, handsome, sturdy and strong with all the right attributes. Now in his leather jacket and nothing else Guy looked more sexy, more himself than ever. This was no costume, no parade. This was Guy Richards. He went to his wardrobe and pulled out a pair of Levi 501's which he rarely wore. Now, pulling the jeans over his bare bum and doing them up save for the top waist button, a most desirable member of the male sex. He put on some running shoes, a pale grey tee-shirt, and feeling complete he left his apartment and wandered into the outside world of Murray Hill. This, Guy decided, was a neighbourhood that no longer interested him, a no man's land without distinct personality. He would move. He would consider the Lower East Side, maybe Brooklyn, New Jersey perhaps, possibly Asbury Park. Guy did not know where he would move but he would.

He walked uptown. He attracted attention. Not obvious attention but admiring glances. He felt good. He definitely felt different.

He purchased a tub of Hagen-Daz chocolate ice-cream from a store. He allowed it to melt in the unkind heat. He drank it as if it were a milkshake. He had never done this before. He had certainly changed.

After striding along for about forty minutes he arrived at a little square opposite the Plaza Hotel on the borders of Central Park. He sat down for a while. He received many smiles. He watched the comings and goings, the activity, the idlers and was amused to be sitting there. He should be at work and he wasn't. Good. Things were going well.

He became fascinated by the behaviour of an eccentric tramp in a black wig, carrying his life around about him and in a state of incessant monologue. Nobody seemed interested in him with the exception of a young woman. A beautiful looking girl, if a little strange, almost with this man though not quite. She hung on his every word and occasionally broke into a fit of laughter at something he said. She lit up when this laughter surrounded her, becoming vivacious, a real beauty. Guy enjoyed them. They were an interesting couple. He watched them for a full hour.

Guy thought of nothing, no anxiety, no guilt, no future plans. He liked this, this was a new experience. When the couple moved on he followed.

It was eight fifteen when Guy realised the time. He had been behind or nearby these two characters all afternoon and evening. They had been to the Metropolitan Museum and hung around on the steps. They had wandered into Central Park and crossed to the

Upper West Side. And then a remarkable thing had occurred; they arrived at the very crematorium where James' service was held. They had waited outside for a good half hour or more watching mourners come and go.

They had gone to a coffee shop and the young woman bought coffee and pastries for her and her companion. Guy stayed close by without entering their company. They knew he was about but they did not seem unduly concerned.

He was now at Columbus Circle remembering his dinner date with Alexandra and Anne-Marie in fifteen minutes time. "Damn," he thought, he ought to have arrived first to introduce them, then, "Damn them, let them meet themselves."

He yearned to ask the couple he had followed to join him for dinner but lacked the courage. He rode the subway, something he had not done for seven years, down to Greenwich Village. He arrived at the restaurant at ten past nine. The train had remained stationary under the darkest tunnel for an enjoyable twenty minutes. Seven years without the subway and this was his fate. Had an engine roared too loudly? Had a suicide jumped? He neither knew nor cared. Nor cared that he was forty minutes late for his date. Nor concerned with the way he was dressed. The restaurant they were to dine in qualified as fashionable as opposed to chic so he passed muster in his present mufti. He fully expected the two women to be staring at one another, separated by twin martinis and struggling to settle upon suitable topics of conversation. He could not have been more wrong.

Firstly they were sitting in a booth side by side, drinking Dom Perignon and above all talking so furiously that they were almost huddled together. When Guy apologised for his tardiness they took little if any notice and apart from Anne-Marie commenting slyly on his dress neither woman seemed at all affected by his absence, even less preoccupied with his presence.

It transpired that Alexandra and Anne-Marie had previously met. Anne-Marie was the woman toying with the idea of buying Alexandra's apartment.

Guy had rarely seen Anne-Marie so animated. He wanted to tell them about his new friends, his past days, his excursion, but they were inclined to exclude him and continue with their private conversation.

Alexandra did not even enquire about his health, having last seen him a ghostly figure at his bathroom door.

Guy picked his way through chilled cucumber soup, rack of lamb and apple crumble, while he fantasised where life would lead him next.

The two women ordered another bottle of Dom Perignon and ate hardly anything. Guy did not drink.

The only time the coversation included all three people was an alarming moment when Anne-Marie ventured: "I saw the most curious advertisement in the New York Times yesterday. I noticed it because it mentioned the name James but I couldn't help feeling that you were involved Guy. Am I mad?" "Isn't that extraordinary?" piped up Alexandra, "*I* noticed it because it mentioned Tangier and it made me think of Guy."

Guy, a small piece of lamb lodging firmly in his gullet, was absolutely horrified. In an attempt to contact his saviour he had managed to communicate with exactly the wrong people. Feeling utterly miserable he turned down his lower lip like a sulking child and said:

"What?"

"Did you..." started Anne-Marie "...oh never mind." And the ladies set off again, basking in each other.

After such a pleasant day this awful dinner was depressing him and then a tiny event happened to lift his spirits: through the restaurant window, situated next to their table, he could spy his chums, the man with the wig and the young woman. They settled a few paces from the restaurant and huddled together on the pavement.

Guy was delighted. He could barely touch his apple crumble. He could hardly wait to pay the bill and be on his way. The ladies wanted coffee and considered a liquer but Guy forced the issue saying he must go and suggesting they take coffee back at Anne-Marie's without him. The bill was sent for and after much haggling over who should pay, each one feeling they owed everybody else something, they went dutch. Anne-Marie was a little startled and looked at Guy through new eyes. She had not seen him socially for a while and had promised herself to examine him more carefully when she did next see him, and now she had spent the evening without paying him any attention whatsoever. Still . . . she returned herself to the Argentinian and the girls started a whole new conversation.

Guy guided them out of the restaurant and said his goodbyes. Alexandra and Anne-Marie did not notice anything: did not notice that Guy was still with them saying goodbye rather than *good night*. They were gone, arm in arm, an embrace more than a link, in the direction of the lights, the activity. Guy hesitated for a moment, then taking his courage in a bold embrace he walked toward the twosome.

"Hello," said the young woman, "my name's Rosemary."

"Hello. I'm Guy."

"Yes I know. This is the Wigman."

The Wigman laughed.

"Mind if I join you?"

"We've been waiting for you."

Rosemary and the Wigman got to their feet.

"Come on. Let's go," she said.

"Where?"

"Who knows?"

They started towards the Hudson, the streets ahead of them looking dark and deserted.

"Where do you sleep?" asked Guy.

The Wigman laughed.

"We don't," replied Rosemary.

Nervously, almost longingly, Guy walked next to them, almost on tip-toe.

The three walked, without purpose, past block after block, into a part of the city so dark they seemed to disappear altogether.